THE MEDICINE MAN CROSSED HIS ARMS ACROSS his chest and did not reply. Straight he looked into the muzzle of the ready gun, and Messenger vainly gritted his teeth. He could not shoot the defenseless man.

He lowered the gun again and began to curse, softly, behind his teeth. Summer Day merely smiled.

"You have a knife and a gun," he said, "but after a moment, you will throw them both away, and will fight me evenly, with your bare hands."

At this, Messenger laughed aloud. "What would I gain, except a chance to fight a much bigger man?"

"You would gain the one thing that you really want, a chance to feel me dying between your hands."

Messenger drew in a great breath, then hurled the revolver far from him. After the gun, he threw his knife. Then he made a gesture with both of his empty hands.

"Are you ready, Summer Day?"

\*     \*     \*     \*     \*

"[Brand's] characters . . . are figures belonging more to myth . . . they materialize in prose glittering with detail, heated by emotion . . . in a world more open, more dangerous, more intense than our familiar present."

—Robert Sampson, author of *Yesterday's Faces: A Study of Series Characters in the Early Pulp Magazines*

# MOUNTAIN GUNS

WARNER BOOKS

A Warner Communications Company

WARNER BOOKS EDITION

This Warner Books Edition is published by arrangement
with Dodd, Mead & Company, Inc., 79 Madison Avenue,
New York, N.Y. 10016

*Mountain Guns* was first published in *Western Story Magazine*
in six installments in 1930 under the title of *Trouble's Messenger*,
written under the name of George Owen Baxter.

Warner Books, Inc.
666 Fifth Avenue
New York, N.Y. 10103

A Warner Communications Company

Printed in the United States of America

First Warner Books Printing: August, 1986

10  9  8  7  6  5  4  3  2  1

# 1

Now Louis Desparr was content.

For twenty years he had been laboring, trading, hauling, packing, portaging, fighting, and all that he had made from that generation of work was enough to give him one good stock of trade goods. That was when he determined to build Fort Lippewan.

Louis was not only determined, but he was methodical. He believed in hard fighting, but he believed in generalship, also.

First of all, he decided that he would give up the wandering life of the trapper and select a spot for stationary trading. Then he hunted through the list of possibilities which was stocked in his memory. And, when he came in his list to the Lippewan River, his eyes rolled upward in sudden reflection. He could see the point where the two tributary streams ran into the Lippewan. He could see the point where the rocky bluff advanced well out from the shore, naturally defended by its clifflike steepness and height, on two sides of its triangular shape. The other side, the base of the little peninsula, was narrow. Sometimes, at high water, a current ran across the neck, and the peninsula became a little island. But in any time or case, the site was eminently defensible. The projecting point was crowded with a heavy growth of timber. Down the river and its two tributaries, the Indians and the white mountain men could paddle their canoes with very few portages, and those only on the head waters. They could follow a natural road down to the fort. For that was where he built it.

He had to do two things.

First, since the country was in the land of the Blackfeet, and he was not a great friend of theirs—having taken a Piegan scalp or two in his happy younger days—he must have a way of cementing a friendship between himself and that tribe.

This he managed, at an easy stroke, by taking as squaw-wife, Dancing Shadow, the daughter of the war chief, Angry Child. There was nothing pretty about Dancing Shadow, except her name. When her features were young and tender, she had been kicked in the midst of them, and they were rather mixed together as a result. One eye pulled down and one eye pulled aside. She was always looking two ways at once. Her face was so deformed that not even the thick-skinned Blackfeet bucks could persuade themselves to take her as a squaw, even as a gift.

Proud Angry Child consumed his heart with disappointment, and grew so tired of the sight of his daughter's face that the very bones of his head ached when he so much as looked at her. Then arrived the trader, Louis Desparr, half English, half French. Or was there a little strain of Indian blood already in him? He did not want a beauty. He was past the age of romance, and merely asked for a worker. Dancing Shadow was as strong as an ox, and built very much like one. She stood six feet tall; she was made solidly, and based on huge feet. And when the trader saw her, he could tell at a glance that she would be faithful, and never mysterious. So he took her. Not as a gift. He got together some horses, beads, and guns, and gave the handsome lot to Angry Child, who was almost persuaded that it had been worthwhile to wait even as long as this!

The gift was a master stroke. It restored to Dancing Shadow her self-respect. It warmed the heart of Angry Child. And it established in the minds of the Indians that this was a rich and generous white man, apt to be a little foolish in driving a bargain. All of this seed would assuredly bear fruit a hundredfold.

Then Louis Desparr went with his wife down to the junction of the streams, and for a whole year they labored at the building of the fort. The two of them felled, trimmed, and squared trees into logs, and ran a redoubtable palisade across the neck of the peninsula. When a party of Dancing Shadow's relatives and friends stopped by to visit with her, Desparr got their help in the hoisting of the main timbers, and once the skeleton of the buildings which was to compose the fort had been established, it was comparatively easy for him and Dancing Shadow to build up the walls and do the roofing.

They toiled without a pause until the task was almost completed. Then he left her there alone, with a rifle for company, and went off down the river. He came back with all the trading stock that he could get together by spending his last cent, and mortgaging his future to the hilt. Then word was sent out to the tribes, and presently they began to come in.

They still were coming.

They brought in great piles of beautifully tanned buffalo robes. They brought in any quantity of beaver skins. They brought in their herds of horses, too. There were suits worked with colored quilts, and others heavily incrusted with beads until they were almost like suits of chain mail. Sometimes they carried in painted robes which were true works of art. Often they had ornamented back rests, willow beds in rolls, baskets, pottery. And, whatever they brought, the careless Louis Desparr always was willing to buy or trade for—at a price.

3

Having once made up their minds, Indians do not readily change them. And so, when Desparr gained the repute of being a rather foolishly generous price maker, the repute clung to him long after he began to drive the sharpest of bargains. Beaver skins and buffalo robes were what he wanted, but he would take anything he could get and put it in his stores, until he had a chance to trade back with it. He gave the red men beads, mirrors, knives, guns, lead, gunpowder, pins, needles, axes and hatchets, and he always had tea, sugar, coffee, and trade whisky. The last was an abomination composed of sheer grain alcohol, afterward compounded with coloring matters and greatly diluted. There was a punch in this liquor which was not altogether that of alcohol. But it was a very popular drink with the Indians. Obviously, a liquid which drives a brave mad with half a pint is twice as good as "whisky" of which one can consume a quart before beginning to stagger.

Louis Desparr traded every morning from dawn to high noon. Then he closed up his stores. The Indians were invited to wander where they pleased, but there was no trading in the fort of an afternoon.

The squaw, Dancing Shadow, took charge of the stock and guarded it with her two-direction eyes, which saw all things in a single glance, as it appeared. With such a shepherd, sheep would hardly be stolen.

And Louis Desparr was left free to conduct more important items of his affairs. For instance, he could interview the influential warriors and the big chiefs. He could chat with visitors from more distant tribes and invite them to come to this haven of just prices and good stock. He could estimate the importance of the men to whom he must give presents, and hit upon the heart's desire of each one.

That was the secret of Desparr's success.

He began to dispatch boatloads of furs in blunt-nosed, flat-bottomed skiffs that could be poled or sailed downstream. And, for every half dozen or more of these, a narrow canoe would come nosing up the river, keeping to the shallows, delayed only by a few short portages, and tugged by horses up to the fort.

There, at Fort Lippewan, the stocks were unloaded, and so the trading went merrily on.

Desparr, beginning at bedrock, already had cleaned up thousands of dollars in a single season, and a good part of that season was still to run!

No wonder that he was content as he sat on the flat roof of his main building with Henry Lessing, the hunter and trapper, both of them smoking long-stemmed pipes. The tobacco was so good—having just arrived, and being in the height of its unspoiled strength and richness of flavor—that now and again, drawing a long whiff, they half-closed their eyes. Henry Lessing was an old acquaintance. Now he looked at the bustle below them, where the crowds of children, squaws, and braves were passing and repassing, with a few white men of various kinds mixed among them. He looked at this bustle and nodded.

"You're gunna get rich, Louis," said he.

"You'll do this, one day," said Louis.

"I ain't a thinker," said the other, very frankly.

He waved his hand beyond the palisade, where the Indian encampments were spread. There were three distinct sections of three distinct Blackfeet tribes then present. And so commodious was the land that there was plenty of space for all of them to have camps where water and wood would be easy to get at, and where there was open country, besides, to race their horses, and to play their games. Voices came shouting faint and far from the open land. Some young men were flogging half a dozen ponies as they raced out to a rock and back around it. Their long hair streamed out behind them.

Lessing again looked down into the yard of the fort.

5

"There's the tenderfoot again," said he.

"Which one?" said the trader.

"The one that can talk the Blackfoot language."

"Is he still hunting?"

"Still hunting," said Lessing. "Still looking at faces. Have you found out what he wants?"

"He won't talk," said Louis Desparr. "He'll only look."

And, as though the subject were irresistibly interesting, he leaned forward until he could see the man in question.

It was not hard to pick out the stranger.

In the first place, where all the others were in motion, he stood fast at the corner of the storehouse, with his arms folded. In the second place, their skins were dark. The other whites had lived so long and so much like Indians, that they were almost as bronzed as the braves themselves. But this lad was flushed rather than stained by the sun. Besides, the others were dressed in neatly fitted deerskins. But the white boy was in a rough, gray cloth.

"What could he be?" said Louis Desparr, almost gloomily.

"I dunno," answered Henry Lessing. "He's as straight as an Indian."

"He's as blond as a Swede," said Louis.

"He's got a pair of arms and a set of shoulders onto him."

"When he finds what he's lookin' for, there'll be trouble."

"Trouble for the tenderfoot, I reckon."

"He might be a first-class fightin' man," said the other.

After a moment of reflection, Louis Desparr added: "Look here, Henry. How is it that he knows how to talk good Blackfoot? Not like you and me, but the real lingo, like he was raised with it."

"Maybe he was, then."

"But all that he knows about the Blackfeet is their lingo."

"Yeah, he's a tenderfoot, all right. Won't he ever talk none?"

"Not a bit, to nobody," said Desparr. "He acts like he thought that he was a duke."

They went on with their smoking, still staring fixedly at the stranger.

"He's looking for trouble," insisted Lessing. "One of them Indians is gunna pass half a foot of knife between his ribs, if he keeps on starin' at every face, with that sneer of his."

"Maybe he don't mean nothing," said the trader. "He's too young to know much."

"Aye, that's true. He's pretty young. I'd hate to be that young again, Louis. It makes me feel pretty chilly even to think of being such a kid again. Like jumping off into ice water."

"Aye," nodded Desparr. "It's a hard thing—in this part of the world."

"Did you ever ask that boy a straight question about what brought him here?"

"No. I ain't a question-asker. I listen when I get a chance, but him that asks questions is askin' for lies."

"He needs to have some questions asked," said the other.

"Not by me. He's looking for a man, that's what he's looking for."

Now, suddenly, the trapper stood up.

He was a tall, lean fellow of nearly fifty, iron gray, hard

and tough as bull's hide from constant living in the open. He was dressed in deerskin trousers, but they were old, and fitted rather loosely. And he wore a blue-flannel shirt, which had faded over the shoulders to a meager tan. His hair was clipped off short across his brow, and descended in a matted, unkempt tangle to the base of his neck, behind. He wore what had once been a white belt of the skin of a mountain goat, but the original color had become grimy and hand-worn. On one side it supported a great knife in a sheath. On the other side was a double pouch to contain ammunition and tobacco. On his feet were clumsy but comfortable moccasins. And it was plain that no man in the world cared less about appearances than did Henry Lessing.

"I'm gunna go down and talk to that boy," said he.

"I wouldn't do it," declared Desparr. "He wouldn't thank you, and he wouldn't talk."

"Hold on!" said Lessing, raising his hand.

A party of three or four young braves, at that moment, was passing the corner at which the stranger stood, and one of them, stumbling or pretending to stumble, fell heavily against the tenderfoot. The shock knocked him from his place and sent him reeling several paces.

He who had stumbled did not stay to apologize. He went on with his companions, and their grins were very broad indeed.

"Now what'll the boy do?" asked Lessing, muttering to himself.

"Nothing!" exclaimed Desparr. "He's yellow, Henry. Look at that!"

For the stranger, recovering from the blow, calmly resumed his former position at the angle of the building and continued to look at the passers-by.

"Yellow as a dog!" repeated Desparr.

"Aye—maybe!" said Lessing.

8

"The word of that'll get around," said Desparr. "There won't be any peace for that tenderfoot, from now on. Every half-growed-up buck in the tribe will try to step on his toes!"

"What's his name?"

"He calls himself Peter Messenger."

"Well, Messenger will have trouble anyway. He's made for trouble. There never was a man from the beginning of time with a chin like that, that wasn't made for trouble. But yaller? I dunno about that!!"

"You'll see. They'll try the same dodge again on him."

"If I was them, I wouldn't."

"You think he's something?"

"Kind of by an itch in my bones, I do."

Desparr chuckled.

"It's that worthless Dust-in-the-sky," he observed. "He's always around raising a ruction. There ain't any peace when that young buck is about."

"He'll lose his hair, one of these days."

"He's got some hair already drying in his teepee," answered Desparr. "Comanche hair, at that. He loves a fight, does that Dust-in-the-sky."

"And maybe he'll get it."

"Not out of the tenderfoot."

"Would you bet on that, Louis?"

"I'll bet. What you want to bet on it?"

"You took a fancy to that pinto mare that I rode in."

"Hey, Henry, are you gunna bet that mare on a greenhorn that you never seen before?"

"I been doin' a lot of thinkin' about that greenhorn," said Lessing. "I'll bet the mare. What'll you bet?"

"What you want?"

"I seen one of those new Colt revolvers down in the store. How about that?"

"It's a mighty expensive gun," said the trader cautiously.

"I'll throw in my saddle, too," said Lessing calmly.

Louis Desparr shrugged. "This is after business hours, anyway," said he. "The gun agin' the mare, if you want to. But you're gunna lose. What do you expect? That he'll follow Dust-in-the-sky, or that the buck will come back to him?"

"The buck will come back to him. He's got the taste in his teeth, now, and he'll try to bully the white man. You'll see, Louis!"

"Aye, I'll see."

"There comes Dust, now!"

The same party returned, recruited to seven or eight. They wore an appearance of innocent absent-mindedness.

As the group came nearer, one of the other young bucks stumbled exactly as Dust-in-the-sky had done before, and fell toward the white man.

Then Peter Messenger moved. He sidestepped with a gliding speed like that of a cat, caught the young buck as the latter floundered forward, and turning, by a maneuver which even the sharp eye of Desparr could not follow, he flung the Indian over his shoulder.

The latter turned a full half circle in the air and landed with such force that the wind was knocked out of him with a grunt audible to the watchers upon the roof.

He did not rise again, at once.

The dust which had been thrown out in a great puff on either side of his body now steamed upward, and dissolved in the air. But still he did not rise.

"How the dickens did the boy do that?" asked the startled Desparr.

"That's what they call a neck lock," said Henry Lessing. "And if I ain't badly mistaken, young Mr. Blackfoot is gunna have a stretched neck and a sore head for a spell. I never seen that trick done better."

"It was neat! It was mighty neat!" said Desparr, in generous admiration. "I didn't expect nothin' like that. But there is Dust-in-the-sky goin' in to finish up the job!"

That young brave stepped straight up before the white man and uttered something in an angry voice, but the white man paid no heed to him at all. Oblivious of his presence, he stared past the Indian toward the more distant faces in the crowd that drifted by.

"Look, look, look!" said Desparr, greatly excited now. "Seems to me like a real man has arrived out here at Fort Lippewan!"

"Aye," said Henry Lessing. "I reckoned that before. If Dust-in-the-sky makes a move to touch him, there'll be another explosion. Is Dust-in-the-sky that much of a fool that he can't tell gunpowder when he sees it?"

The voice of Dust-in-the-sky rose higher, with a savage snarl in it. That fighting sound stopped every passer-by, and, from a distance, men came running to enjoy the possible fight.

"Stop it, Desparr!" exclaimed Henry.

"Let 'em have it out," said the trader philosophically. "Bad blood needs the air. As long as they don't start fighting inside my store, they can do what they please when the sky is over their heads!"

"Well," said Lessing, "if it comes to a pinch, I'm sorry for the Blackfoot."

# 3

So convinced was he of the tenderfoot's superiority, that he actually turned his head and looked away from his preferred champion to the flash of the sun on the river. Across the open land to the south, he could see a dust cloud. It had been approaching for some time, and with such incredible slowness that he could only guess at an ox team and at least two wagons in the train.

"There it goes!" gasped Desparr, with a chuckle of pleased excitement.

He had been so long among scenes of violence that bloodshed meant almost nothing to him. A man had to take his chances as he found them. And, after all, life cannot last forever.

As for Lessing, he glanced down in time to see the glittering of steel in the hand of Dust-in-the-sky. That flash leaped at the throat of the white man, but again Peter Messenger moved.

He stepped just enough aside to allow the gleam of the knife to shoot harmlessly over his shoulder. And he stepped just enough in to bring him to comfortable short-arm distance. Then he snapped a hard fist up to the point of the brave's chin.

Dust-in-the-sky was a brave young man. And he was as tough as twenty-five summers and winters of mountain hunting and mountain fighting could make him. But a bell had been rung in his brain with a dull buzz like a swarm of bees. His wits scattered upon the winds. He went backward, like one who cannot get his balance, and after floundering a few steps, he sank to the ground in a loose, helpless pile, his head slumping down upon his knees.

"He had the shoulders," said Lessing critically, and apparently unmoved by this victory, which he had prophesied. "He had the shoulders, and it looked like he had the arms. But he's got the science, too. He's been trained well.

"Watch, now. There's something more coming. They're gunna mob him!"

The group had swayed threateningly in toward the white man as their leader fell under that stroke. But now they paused for a moment when Messenger leaned and picked from the ground the knife which Dust-in-the-sky had dropped. A big, formidable-looking weapon it was, brand-new from the store of Desparr.

"Hello!" said Desparr. "Does he mean to tackle that band with a knife? They'll cut him to pieces in half a second."

"He won't tackle them. He's defending himself, and that's all," declared Lessing with perfect assurance. "You watch him, Louis."

The hand of Messenger rose with the knife and then flicked it away with a swift and graceful motion. It turned over once in the sunshine, and then landed just between the knees and an inch from the scalp lock of Dust-in-the-sky, burying its blade to the hilt in the ground.

Desparr jumped up with an exclamation. "Did you see that, Henry?" he asked.

Lessing merely smiled, as though he were hearing a twice-told tale.

"He had the shoulders and the arms. He has the fingers, too," said he. "There's nothing green about that boy but his skin, Louis!"

13

"There go the Blackfeet. They've had enough of that fellow's medicine, and I don't blame them!"

The group of young braves, in fact, had withdrawn a few steps, hastily, and some of them picked up their fallen leader.

They supported him as they went off.

But he was still in dreamland, his face blank, his mouth open, and his feet trailing.

"What a punch!" said Desparr enthusiastically. "An iron hand, Henry. I couldn't do that with a club, let alone a bare fist!"

"See what the boy's doing now," answered Lessing.

The tenderfoot, stepping back to his chosen place of vantage, had folded his arms again and remained exactly as he had been before—his head high, his eye constantly traveling over the faces of the crowd which, by this time, was closely packed about him.

A white trapper stepped from the semicircle and slapped him cordially on the shoulder. And the two on the rooftop could hear the boy being invited to take a drink.

His answer was a mere shake of the head, and the trapper drew back, with a black scowl. The crowd, at this, rapidly melted away, only a little half-naked Indian boy remaining to gape up at this newly found hero.

"There you are," said Lessing. "That boy has made three enemies in two minutes, and every one of the three would like to have his blood, especially Beaver Jones."

"Beaver's no good," said Desparr. "I'm glad that the boy could see through him."

Lessing chuckled.

"I'll tell you, old friend," said he, "that the boy wouldn't drink because he doesn't know that stranger. He wants an introduction, before he'll take a drink with a man."

"Aye, or else he don't drink."

14

"Not drink?" said Lessing, startled by his suggestion in a land where all men drank what they could get.

"Maybe," said Desparr, putting out a hand before him in a gesture like that of one who vaguely feels his way toward something of importance, "maybe the business of that boy won't let him fog up his brain with liquor."

Lessing snapped his fingers.

"Aye, maybe you've put your finger on it," said he. "I'd guess that you're right, Louis."

"You've won a brand-new gun, Henry."

"I've won more than that," declared Lessing.

"What else have you won?"

"A good time," declared the trapper. "I ain't seen that kind of man in ten years."

"What kind of man? Fighting man, you mean?"

"Why, the land's full of fighting men, Louis. How could I mean that?"

"I didn't know. What kind of man do you mean?"

"Did you see how he stepped?" asked Lessing.

"He's as fast on his feet as a cat."

"He's a cat," said Lessing with conviction. "It's been ten years since I seen the like of him."

"Who've you got in mind, Henry?"

"There was that Claud Tamlin, but maybe you've forgot him?"

"Nobody that seen Tamlin ever forgot him. You think this kid reminds you of Tamlin?"

"He moved the same way," said Henry Lessing, "and he held his chin up, the same way."

"But Claud Tamlin was three inches shorter, and a foot wider, and six inches deeper. You could've cut three or four of this lad out of Tamlin."

"He's young! He's young!" said Lessing. "But look at that crowd, now!"

"What about it?"

"I've seen people move like that when Tamlin was around; because they always gave him room enough!"

In fact, the casual passer-by now made a wide eddy at the corner of the storehouse, letting the tall young tenderfoot have plenty of elbow room. They did not any longer meet the eye of the youth, either, but pretended to be very occupied with their own business. Though, all the time, it was plain that they were scanning him out of the corners of their eyes. The young braves came by most slowly of all, stalking with consummate dignity—and, doubtless, they were busily measuring the dimensions and noting down the features of this strange fellow.

"I remember Tamlin at Bent's Fort," said Desparr, at last. "I remember him standin' up, and the crowd flowin' around him like water around a rock. He was a rock!"

"Aye, he was a rock, and a wildcat, too."

"He was both them things," agreed Desparr seriously. "What become of Tamlin?" he asked.

"They got him, at last."

"Which tribe?"

"There's a good deal of question about that. Some says that it was old Broken Feather and his Comanches that finished up Tamlin. And some says that it was these here Blackfeet, as far as that goes!"

"Maybe it never happened at all," declared Desparr. "If they got his death scattered that wide apart, maybe it never happened at all."

"Maybe it never did," agreed Henry Lessing. "But he ain't been heard of for years."

"Maybe he's left the land."

"How could he live away from buffalo and Injuns?"

"I dunno. I dunno. Well, are you gunna go down and talk to that youngster, Lessing?"

Lessing nodded. He took off his wide-brimmed hat and passed his hand through his tangled hair.

"You're just likely to be stepping in knee-deep in trouble!" cautioned Desparr.

"That's what I've been thinkin'," said Lessing softly.

But, nevertheless, down he went to the ground.

# 4

Straight down into the compound Lessing went.

The store itself was thickly crowded, still. Through the open door he could hear a sort of babbling song that went up from the crowd inside. Men, and women, and children, they all were handling, exclaiming over, crying out about the articles for sale. But nothing would be stolen even by their clever fingers, for in the background appeared the face of Dancing Shadow, with her double-direction eyes and her weird ugliness. Yet, her expression now made her almost beautiful. For in her hands was all the delegated authority of her husband. She was in importance like a chief among warriors. She could even make small gifts, here and there, to the wife or to the child of some redoubtable figure of the redskins. And she never gave in vain. With that might to give and to receive, she was richly content.

Lessing went on past the store, and almost fell over a pair of Indian lads who, wrestling violently, tumbled out of the doorway of the store, and rolled over and over in the dust.

Weariness came suddenly over Lessing. A wave of disgust for men and their ways passed over him. The furnishings of his own life were simple. A horse and a mule loaded with traps, a bit of tobacco and salt, some tea, ammunition for his rifle, a good new ax, a pair of knives, and he was ready to start his trek through the wilderness until, some day, he saw before him the heads of unknown mountains, like vast monsters holding up their hands to stop him. There he would settle into another year of life, sinking deeper and deeper into the woods, until the voices of the wind and of the rivers cleansed from his mind the sound of human speech, human wranglings. The crowd through which he had to elbow his way depressed him unutterably, but at last he found himself on the edge of the open space that surrounded the tenderfoot, Peter Messenger.

Lessing did not hesitate.

He walked straight up to the youth. There was an odd feeling that the boy grew, as one came nearer to him. From a little distance, he seemed slender, light, made for swift activity rather than for the bearing of burdens. But, close at hand, the dimensions of the shoulders grew. And, from a distance, it seemed a pale, meager face; but near at hand he saw the noble proportions of the forehead and, deep beneath the brows, the gray eyes which were both alert and still.

"Come with me, Messenger," said the trapper curtly, and, turning on his heel, he walked away.

He half smiled, wondering if the boy would do as he was bid. And, to his deep surprise and satisfaction, he was presently aware that the tall youth was stepping lightly after him.

He led straight out through the open gate in the palisade and through the woods to the edge of the water. There he paused, and Messenger stepped out of the trees instantly, to his side. As he came, he looked searchingly into the face of Lessing, and then his glance darkened a little with disappointment.

It was as though he had hoped vaguely that this stranger might prove to be the thing for which he was searching. And, instantly, Lessing knew that the boy was hunting, indeed, for a human face. Messenger, halting at the edge of the water, faced his guide and waited.

"We're alone here for a minute or so," observed Lessing cheerfully. "Though it won't take 'em long to get on the trail, ag'in."

"Who?" asked Messenger.

Lessing watched him, half amused and half surprised.

"You mean you dunno who would want to take your trail, son?"

Messenger shook his head. He maintained this aloof attitude of his without effort. It seemed natural for him to act as though he were of a superior class.

"Well," said Lessing, "d'you know the names of the two bucks that you laid out?"

"No," said Messenger coldly.

"The first one is Spotted Deer. He has a father that's still a warrior in the prime. He has two young uncles, as hard as nails. He has a brother and half a dozen cousins."

"He's a lucky fellow," said Messenger, with his natural sneer.

Lessing nodded.

"Any one of those people would be glad to throw a war spear into you, my lad. Then there's Dust-in-the-sky—"

"Who is he?" Messenger permitted himself to ask.

"Somebody that you'll be sure to hear of again," declared Lessing. "Dust-in-the-sky is the second one—the fellow that you flattened with that left uppercut. Are you left-handed, Messenger?"

"No," said the boy.

Lessing could not help smiling a little.

"The left is the hand they don't expect," he commented. "The point I'm making, though, is that Dust-in-the-sky has even more friends than the other lad. He could easily bring out a dozen men to run you down."

"Very well," answered Messenger. "It's plain that I'll have to take my chances with them."

"You take your chances," said Lessing, "and get a knife through your gizzard."

"Is that all you brought me here to tell me?" asked Messenger.

Lessing was a man who had been through his share of troubles in this world, but now he flushed a little.

"Are you going to stick at that?" he asked.

"At what?" said the boy.

"At being a young, hard-headed fool?" explained Lessing.

Messenger started. His gray eyes, losing some of their indifference, sparkled for an instant, but almost at once they grew dull again. But the trapper felt as though he had seen a wild animal raise its head and look at him.

"I don't know," said Messenger, "what I ought to say to you. I haven't asked for your advice. And I haven't asked to be brought away from the fort, where I was busy."

"Aye, you were busy," agreed the other. "Busy makin' enemies. I never seen nobody make 'em faster."

"How was I making enemies?" asked the boy, a touch of harsh anger appearing in his voice.

"Why, by lookin' over people as though they was horses. Back in your part of the country, maybe it's different. I guess that back there it's good manners to stare at everybody as though they had two heads. But out here it's different. There's a proud lot, out here, young feller. And if you start to handlin' Injuns and Westerners like that with your eyes, you ain't gunna last long."

"No?" inquired Messenger coldly. "I'll have to take my chances in my own way, as I said before, I believe."

"You won't take 'em long," declared Lessing, "because you'll be dead."

He picked up a stone from the bank of the stream and began to juggle it carelessly in his hand.

"Suppose you tell me," asked the boy, "why you're troubling yourself so much about me?"

"You oughta be able to guess."

"No. I don't see what my business has to do with you."

"Well," said the other, "a man can't help bein' interested when he sees a youngster start in lookin' for trouble."

"I'm not looking for trouble," insisted Messenger. "I didn't raise a hand at either of those two Indians until they forced trouble on me."

"You hadn't asked for it, either, I reckon?" asked the trapper.

"What do you mean?"

"I mean this: That you stand there and sneer and stare at everybody."

"I wasn't sneering," said the boy.

"I didn't have no eyes to see you, eh?"

"I'm going back to the fort," said Messenger suddenly, and in impatience.

"Wait a minute," said the other. "Lemme see what's in the brush over there."

Suddenly he flung the stone which he was holding through the face of a tall, dense shrub, at the same time shouting out.

In answer, came several deep-throated, muffled exclamations, and a noise of the bush crackling as people retired through it.

"Maybe the other side of the brush is the same way," suggested Lessing cheerfully.

Messenger, in the meantime, stood up in the attitude of a soldier, stiff and tense, with his hands gripped into fists at his sides. He looked the very picture of a man about to deliver a savage attack.

This picture, Lessing studied with an almost professional interest.

"Are you goin' after them?" he said.

"What do you think?" asked the boy, snapping out the words suddenly.

Lessing grinned.

"D'you ever ask advice in your life before?" he demanded.

All at once the other smiled, and his whole appearance was so marvelously altered by this smile that the trapper marveled at him.

"You're a strange fellow," said the boy.

"Am I?" answered Lessing, in perfect good nature. "Somehow, I was thinkin' the same thing about you."

The boy smiled again.

"I owe you something," he said slowly. "If I'd gone back toward the fort—"

He hesitated. Then he brought the words out one by one, as though his honesty were forcing them through his lips.

"If I'd started back for the fort, they would have had me! In the back, I suppose!"

And he held out his hand toward the older man.

# 5

Henry Lessing, as the strange lad held out his hand, recognized instantly that a great thing was taking place before his very eyes.

He could not help but see that there was far more in that silent gesture than in a thousand words of gratitude from another man. And yet he hesitated to accept the hand which was proffered. Something made him at the last moment draw back, as though there were a realization that, if he dared to become the friend of the tenderfoot, a thousand dangers would instantly be heaped upon his head.

Yet that instinct had only a momentary and hardly noticeable control over him. Then he thrust out his hand and grasped that which was offered to him.

The fingers were long, hard, and cool. They pressed those of Lessing with strength, but not with a foolish use of force. Afterward, Lessing felt as though he had taken a hand of iron in his own.

"Now will you tell me what made you come after me?" asked the boy.

"Because you're young," insisted Lessing, "and because every older man is every younger man's father, in a way."

Young Messenger looked rather quizzically at the other.

"Father?" said he. And then he smiled.

The cold insolence of that smile almost made the trapper strike him in the face.

"Not meanin'," said Lessing angrily, "that I'm the father of any Duke of What-not, like you!"

The youth was not angered by this remark. He accepted it with his accustomed calm.

"You've been kind to me," said he. "You've given me some good advice. I've told you that I thank you. Is there anything else that we ought to say?"

It was like a machine speaking.

"You've added everything up, and there ain't anything left over, I guess," suggested Lessing, suddenly smiling.

"Why do you smile?" asked the boy.

"Why, because you act like such a thing as conversation never existed."

"Ah, you mean that you want to stand here and talk?"

Lessing conquered his first impulse regarding an answer, and he merely said: "There's nothing that I want to do more!"

There was impatience, there was contempt, there was endurance, in the face of the boy.

"Very well," he said, after a moment of struggle, in which it was apparent that he mastered himself even more strongly than the trapper had done. "Very well, you have the right to ask questions, and I certainly shall answer them. Will you begin, sir?"

"Look here," said the trapper. "Who said that I wanted to ask questions?"

"I imagine that this is the ordinary process of conversation."

"Do you?"

"How else can it progress?"

"Why," said the trapper, more and more intrigued, "you could say that that's a whale of a big oak tree, and I could tell you about another I'd seen that was bigger, and with more of a head to it, too. Or you could say how fast the water's runnin' there, and I could tell you the kind of fish that you could catch out of it. If you're interested in fishin'."

"I am not," said the boy coldly.

"Well, I was aimin' to point out what could be said, and no questions asked. You might call that the track of a mule deer, there—"

"I wouldn't," said the boy.

"You wouldn't?" asked the trapper. "And what would you call it, then?"

"I wouldn't attempt to name it. It looks like a cow track to me."

"Cow track?" cried the trapper, almost shouting. "That a cow track? Did you ever see a cow track with such toe prints?"

"I've never looked very closely at a cow track, either," said the boy.

"Cow track my foot!" said Lessing, and even chuckled. "There never was a cow that could make a track like that. Nor a mule deer, neither, for that matter!"

"I suppose you know what you're saying," said the boy.

"D'you think that I don't?"

"I don't presume to criticize. I've never seen a deer, not even its track."

"Jumping, flopping thunderbird!" exclaimed Henry Lessing. "How did you ever get this far north, then? Or this far west, without seeing a deer?"

"By keeping my eyes on the road in front of me."

"By daydreaming you mean to say!"

"You can call it what you please. But I've never seen a deer."

"Never seen one! Never shot one! Why, boy, you ain't lived, hardly!"

This made Messenger look quizzically up through the green gloom of the branches which hung above them.

"I don't know," said he. "I suppose I can fairly say that I

never have, in the sense which you give to the word."

"Set down," said the trapper. "I gotta talk some more to you."

Messenger glanced impatiently down the course of the river, as if he wished urgently to be gone. But again he controlled himself, and slowly he sat down on the edge of a fallen log. Lessing dropped down nearby and, half turning, faced his companion squarely.

"How come that you could use a hunting knife so slick, then?"

The boy hesitated.

"How come," went on Lessing, "that you took a ten-inch knife and handled it like it was understanding what you talked and wanted?"

"I was raised to understand knives and their ways," said the boy.

"How do you mean that you were raised to understand knives and their ways?"

"That's all the explanation that I care to give," said Messenger calmly.

"I'm kind of interested," said the trapper at last, though he had been halted by this rebuff. "I know a little mite about guns and gun work, and knives and knife work, myself. Why would you get to learn about knives if you wasn't going to learn about deer, I'd like to know?"

Messenger considered this for a moment, as though he wondered whether or not he should answer the questions. At last he said: "Well, are knives used on deer only?"

"No, on other varmints. But if you've never seen deer, you've never seen much else that a hunting knife would do you any good on."

"No," said the boy, "I never saw wild life. Just in a zoo, I might say, and a very small zoo, at that."

"My friend," said Lessing, "I never heard nobody talk like you before."

26

This drew no answering comment from the other.

"Lemme find out, will you, what you ever used a knife on before today?"

"Certainly," said Messenger. "I don't see any reason why I shouldn't tell you that. I used it on a strong sack, usually made of canvas, glazed with tar, and stuffed hard with saw-dust."

"Why was that, might I ask?"

"The sack, do you see, was no larger than the round of your arm, and the glazed canvas was so hard and tough that only a knife thrown hard would cut the canvas, and stick in that hard-packed sawdust."

The trapper stared in earnest this time.

"Which I'd gather that you throwed a knife a good deal at a sack, like that?"

"Yes, a good deal."

"And what was you practicin' for, and what made you so hot to stick a knife into a canvas sack, will you tell me, son?"

Messenger allowed a faint smile to touch his compressed lips.

"Suppose you had to throw that knife across the width of a room," said he, "and if you failed to stick it in once in every three times you got five strokes with a half-inch rat-tan across the bare of your back at the end of the day—would that make you interested in getting the knife into the sack?"

Lessing exclaimed. All his free-born American blood boiled suddenly in his veins.

"By the jumping, flopping thunderbird," he cried, breaking out into his favorite oath, "what scoundrel done that to you?"

The eyes of the boy narrowed. He rose from the log.

"I've talked long enough, I feel," said he.

Lessing shook his head.

"That was where you learned to handle a knife, eh? And

the same gent taught you how to use your fists, too?"

"Oh, no," said Messenger. "There was a separate man to teach me that, of course."

"You was taught special! You was taught special!" exclaimed the trapper, highly pleased. "I knowed it when I seen you sidestep. You wouldn't learn how to sidestep like that without special teachin'—steppin' out as though the ground had turned red hot under you. You had a reason for learnin' to step fast, I reckon!"

"Yes," said the boy. "Either step fast, or be knocked down."

And, with rather an absent-minded look, he touched his chin with the tip of a finger. And Lessing noticed, for the first time, a thin white scar curved along the angle of the jaw.

The trapper wanted to ask a hundred questions. He wanted to ask who the person or persons were who were responsible for such treatment of a lad, and who dared to teach a boy to box by knocking him down unless he learned the proper maneuvers and executed them promptly enough. What mysterious tyrant forced his will so implicitly upon a child? Whose brain was it that had hammered and tempered this lad until he was like iron in brain and in body and in hand?

But he saw, at once, that such a rude probing into the past would bring less than no result. He resolved on going about things in a more diplomatic manner.

"I remember hearin' a man by name of Tamlin say that the foundation of good boxin' was a straight left and a side-step."

"And a right cross," said the boy.

"But uppercuts," said the trapper, "they don't grow on every bush."

"Oh, no," replied Messenger. "Let me see—I didn't even try them for six or seven years."

He said it carelessly, as if it were a matter of no impor-tance, but it conjured into the brain of the trapper a picture of a spindling lad with tow head, narrow lips, dancing feet, sparring with some dexterous and maturely developed brute—someone whose blow, if not dodged or parried or blocked, would knock the youngster down—aye, and per-haps cut him to the bone, as that blow on the jaw must have done, years before.

And then, feeling that he had asked about as much as he could gain by direct query, he went on: "Suppose you tell me, stranger, how you're gunna get back to the fort. Them woods might be filled with Injuns. I got an idea that they are."

Young Messenger looked gravely about him at the shrub-bery.

"I could have a look," he said at last.

"How could you have a look, will you tell me?"

"Why, into the bush, of course."

"You're likely to make a lot of noise, wadin' through that brush."

"I won't wade through it," said the boy.

"What will you do, then, if you don't mind me askin'?"

"Why, I'll look over the top of it, like this."

He took two steps, and, jumping up, caught a thick branch with his hands, using the forward impetus of his leap to swing up until his feet were planted on another bough.

Still without making a pause, he unbent the bow of his body with a force that threw him up to grasp another branch, and so, in a moment, he was lost to the astonished sight of the trapper. And this was done so quietly, that there was no more sound than presently a faint rustling, such as the wind might make among the branches.

That thought of a great cat which had first come into his mind as he looked from the roof of the fort down into the compound, at the mysterious young stranger, again leaped back into his mind. Like a cat, indeed, perfect master of its body and its weight, and sure as a cat in all his movements. Lessing himself, staring up at the boughs by means of which the boy had thrown himself upward, felt the speed of his heart redoubled.

All noise ceased from among the upper branches. There was a very considerable pause.

Then a quiet voice said just above Lessing's head: "There must be twenty of them in the woods."

The trapper jumped almost out of his boots and, turning, looked up.

There he could see the head of the boy, appearing at one side of the huge branch of the tree. Messenger was stretched at ease upon the limb.

"How," said the trapper, who was proud of the forest-trained keenness of his senses, "how in the name of heaven did you come down through that tree without makin' no noise?"

The boy smiled and again his face was changed by that unusual expression.

"Suppose you had to walk fifty feet over gravel and pick up your rations right at the back of the man who was waiting there, straining his ears to hear any movement, even a breath, or the least click of a pebble under your foot? If you can make the trip perfectly once in three times, you get something to eat. Otherwise, you wait till the next day. That's one way of learning to walk softly."

"Aye," said the trapper, "and if you're a born cat, it's not so hard to be silent in the trees, either."

The boy swung down from the branch and landed lightly on his feet, with no more sound than a falling shadow. There was simply a flexure of his entire body to lessen the shock of his feet against the ground. And Lessing would have asked more questions about that feat, also. But he restrained himself. Some time, if all went well, he would be able to draw the whole story from the lips of the boy.

"There are twenty, are there?" asked the trapper, frowning as his thoughts left the boy and concentrated on the danger of their position.

"Yes."

"Where are they?"

"They're stretched in a semicircle from one bank of the water to the other."

"What will you do, if you're left to yourself, to get out of this?" asked the trapper.

"I might go up into the tree and shoot a few of them. I suppose I have a right to shoot my way out?"

"Start shooting, against twenty Indians?"

"Well," said the boy, as calmly as before, "they have cornered us, I suppose."

"Where's your gun? You ain't got one, have you?"

The boy opened his coat and showed a glimpse of a holster slung from the shoulders and hanging at his left side.

"Is that a pistol?"

"It's a revolver."

"At the first shot, you might get one of 'em, but the rest of 'em would hide in that brush like snakes in long grass, and they'd soon begin stalking you."

31

"I ought to get three or four of them, I think," said Messenger thoughtfully. "Several of them are quite a few steps from any cover, considering the angle that I'd have for shooting down at them. Three or four, perhaps even more."

Lessing moistened his dry lips. "That is pretty fast snap shooting," said he.

"Fast?" said the boy. "Well, that depends. Fast snap shooting?" He shook his head.

"You wouldn't call it that?" said the trapper curiously, and half wondering if, after all, there were a good deal of the braggart in the youth.

"Well," said the boy, "I've never shot at a man, before today. But I suppose I'll have to begin sooner or later, out here. All I know is that when you throw six apples into the air and try to get them all with six shots—"

"Have you done that?" cried Lessing, little points of gooseflesh forming all over his body.

"No," said the boy. "I never got more than five at a time. I never could get the sixth one. One shot I was sure to miss, or else I was slow, and one of them hit the ground before I could shoot."

He shook his head again, and his brow contracted. It was plain that he did not relish the memory of that repeated defeat. But Lessing was thinking of six little apples, spinning and winking in the air, and the rapid chatter of shots which must have exploded into the midst of them, smashing them to crisp fragments, one by one, until five of the six were gone. No wonder that the lad was able to calmly estimate that he could get three or four of the Blackfeet from the height of the tree.

"Well," said Lessing, "suppose the shooting were out of the question. Could you do anything then, to get out of the way?"

"The river, of course," said the boy.

"B-r-r! It's ice water, and that current is running along this bank like a galloping horse. Look at that!"

He threw in a small twig. It shot along for a few yards, and then was twisted under the surface by a downward current.

The boy nodded.

"It would be a good hard swim," said he. "But I've no doubt that I could make it, all right. I'm used to cold water. It wouldn't take my breath. I suppose that's what you mean?"

"Aye," said the trapper. "But I'll tell you this, Messenger. If you can handle yourself in that water, you're as good a water dog as any Indian. However, you won't have to shoot your way out of this corner, and you won't have to swim out. Maybe you can guess why?"

Messenger looked steadily at him.

"You wouldn't have brought me out here," he replied at last slowly, "if you could not get me back again."

"Thanks!" grunted the trapper. "No, I certainly ain't that kind of a skunk. Listen, now and—"

He raised his head, and filled his lungs to shout, but at that moment, oddly enough, a roar of voices sounded from across the trees and the open, rolling ground beyond, at the neck of the Fort Lippewan peninsula. It formed itself into a rolling cry, like a cheer. Wild war whoops accompanied it. And suddenly those shouts were reechoed from among the very trees in front of Messenger and his companion.

"By the jumpin', lyin' thunderbird!" cried the trapper. "Did you hear that name they're all shouting? It's War Lance himself that's come!"

# 7

"War Lance? War Lance?" said the boy curiously. "Who is he?"

"Come, come!" said the trapper. "You don't know much about the West, and that's a fact, and about the mountains a pile less, but you've sure heard about War Lance?"

"Not a word, that I remember. Is he a big medicine man?"

"His medicine is big, but he's not a medicine man," said the other. "He's a chief, and for once they saddled one of their heroes with a right name. They've a way of calling their best braves something like Speckled Antelope, or Deer-that-jumps, or some such thing. But War Lance is what this fellow is. Straight as a lance, and as sharp and as strong! You've never heard of War Lance?"

"No. D'you think those Blackfeet in the woods are going to see him?"

"They'll see him," said Lessing, "if they have to swim a river full of floating ice. Of course they'll see him! He's the main trump, the big card, the great smoke in their whole nation. Of course they'll see him!"

"Good luck and a quick trip to them, then!" said the boy carelessly. "I'm glad to do without them, just now. I didn't relish the idea of a swim in that water yonder."

"I could have talked you through them," said Lessing. "They know me, and they're not a bad lot."

Here Messenger turned sharply on him.

"Not a bad lot?" said he. "Not a bad lot? What do you call badness, when they were out there waiting to stick a knife into me?"

"You'd floored a pair of 'em, youngster!"

"With my hands—man to man!" said the boy fiercely. "What would you have had me do?"

"Something dignified, Messenger. An Injun has a pile of dignity, and he hates to have it roughed around. You remember that, if you're going to be cut out here long."

"Aye," said Messenger, with a quick, deep sigh. "I'll be here the rest of my life, I suppose."

"What? The rest of your life? Without going back to the East?"

Lessing never had seen, he felt, a spirit so little in tune with the great Western land.

"I've got to try a thing," said the boy, half to himself, "that I never can do, and it'll take me my life—"

He made a gesture at the trees, and then at the river.

"Among these eternal, gloomy woods," he said, "and ruffians eating dried buffalo meat, drinking poisonous whisky, fighting, brawling, stealing, trailing, freezing, mildewed, ragged, miserable every day of the year, in one way or another. That's the life that lies in front of me!"

He stopped. He flushed hotly and drew himself up.

"I've been complaining, and to a stranger," said he. "I beg your pardon, Mr. Lessing."

Lessing nodded at him with an understanding eye.

"It looks all rank and raw to you," he said. "You'd rather be back there where you could have a good, comfortable chair and a flock of books around you, and polite folks in for tea, and so this part of the woods looks sort of miserable to you, don't it?"

"It does. It does look miserable!" declared the boy. "But I've talked too much. I'm sorry!"

He strode straight ahead, through the brush, and as he went, Lessing struggled to keep up, calling out: "Keep an eye about you. You can't tell about these red men. One of 'em might be hanging back around here to shoot an arrow or a slug into your ribs. It'd be like that Dust-in-the-sky, for one!"

"Good fellows! Good fellows!" quoted the boy, in disgust. "You say that I should have handled them with dignity. How would you have done it, then?"

He paused, and looked haughtily back at Lessing.

"I'll tell you," said Lessing. "I would simply have handled him so that he wouldn't have been made a fool. If I could do what you can with a knife—which I can't—I would never have put a hand on either of them, but I would have fetched out my knife and driven it into the ground right between their toes. That's what I should have done!"

"What would have happened then?"

"That's simple. Only one thing could have happened. They would have seen that you weren't simply a tenderfoot, as they took you to be, but a heap big warrior and brave. Dust-in-the-sky wouldn't have touched that knife, but one of his friends would have pulled it out of the ground, and he would have brought it to you. That would have been the challenge, and you would name your time to meet Dust-in-the-sky out there in the plains, in the pink of some morning when nobody else was up, except a few friends."

"A few friends to help take my scalp, eh?" asked the boy, in his hard, suspicious way.

"You don't understand. You would have been the guest of the Blackfoot nation while that fight was going on. No one would have dared to interfere, except some old war chief, some great man—like this same fellow, War Lance. He might have ridden out and gone to see you. He might have made you a friendly speech and declared that young men should not come to blood for the sake of a joke and such stuff. He might have made you a present of some kind—even a horse, perhaps—and that would have been the end of it."

"I wouldn't take the chance of fighting," answered Messenger most unexpectedly.

"You wouldn't take the chance?" echoed the other, bewildered.

"No. I wouldn't take the chance of fighting. I've no desire to turn into a murderer."

"No question of murder," replied Lessing. "It would be a fair fight."

"How would the fight go?"

"On horseback, with a full equipment. He'd probaby come out as if for the warpath, with a rifle, and a lance, and a knife, and all that. Perhaps there would be a pistol tucked into his belt."

"Well," said the boy gravely, "if I fought him with a rifle, a pistol, a knife, or hand-to-hand, it would still be a murder."

"What?" cried Lessing.

"I was raised for it, trained for it," replied Messenger. "What right have I to fight with ordinary men? They know no more about weapons than babies do about books. It would be simply a murder. That's why I used my bare hands on them. I was sorry I showed the knife at all, but just then I lost my temper. I wanted to go after the whole bullying crowd of them, and I controlled myself just in the nick of time, and shot the knife into the ground, instead."

He said this rapidly. His raising and training were not things on which he cared to linger, very obviously.

Lessing rapped his knuckles against his forehead.

"Maybe you're right," said he. "Maybe you're right, my lad. But—let's get on out of here into the open. You'll forget your troubles if you see War Lance."

They went on rapidly through the woods, until there was a light crackling sound in front of them, and Messenger bounded far to the side, behind a tree. Lessing did not follow the example, but he brought his rifle to the ready, and stared fixedly among the leaves.

"It's nothing," he said presently. "There's no danger that they'll jump you. Listen to the uproar outside. No Indian could prefer his little revenge to the chance of looking at such a party as they have going on out there."

Messenger nodded, and they went on again, with Lessing biting his lip. He had a sudden feeling that this youngster who walked so lightly beside him was a mass of gun powder, ready to blow up a forest, a village, in a single flare.

From the edge of the woods they could get a clear view across the rolling grounds at the base of the peninsula, and there they saw that the entire Indian population was pouring out from the distant woods and swirling into a mass which straightened before their eyes into a line.

This line was made of mounted warriors. To the rear formed a cloud of women and children on foot, and little boys galloped wildly back and forth on their mustangs.

Lessing began to chuckle softly, but there was excitement in his face also.

"You're gunna see a real man, even if his skin isn't white, my son," said he.

They headed, now, straight across toward the narrow of the peninsula base, where the palisade of the fort was strung, and where the gate opened. To that gate, all the occupants of the fort had come in order to see the procession arrive. Some thronged in the gateway itself. Others were grouped on either side, and on the roof of the fort it could be seen that the tarpaulin had been taken from the little ancient brass three-pounder which stood there, its mouth trained straight toward the gate.

"That's loaded with powder only," said Lessing, in explanation, "but if there's a need, it wouldn't take long to slap three-four handfuls of shot into the innards of it and blow a whole lane of those Blackfeet out through that gate and into the happy hunting grounds."

They came up the last slope, hurrying their steps, and as they arrived at the verge of the fort, they could see that the procession which had been forming on the hillside had begun to move.

At the same time, there was a wild babel of shouts, war whoops, and thunderings upon drums. This first blast of outcry ended as abruptly as it had begun, and the procession continued with dignity upon its march.

# 8

First of all, came eight warriors in two ranks. They were naked to the waist, but their deerskin trousers were trimmed and beaded in the height of Indian magnificence. Their belts supported knives and pistols, and even a revolver, here and there, though that weapon had not yet been extensively adopted among the tribes. They were literally brilliant with paint, streaked upon them in rude designs and patterns, which were modified according to the emblems or the personal taste of each hero. They carried long war spears, their rifles being consigned to saddle holsters, or else tied on behind the leg of the rider. These lances were decorated with ruffles, collars, and long streamers of eagle feathers, dyed in the most startling colors. Several had woven the stained feathers together, so that the light banners reached almost to the ground.

All of these men, to judge by their headdresses, were celebrities who had counted many and many a coup, and certainly they had taken many scalps, for the eagle feathers crowned them, and flowed down their backs even beneath the ends of their long hair. This garlanding of spear and head and hair with feathers, to say nothing of others which decorated the ponies, gave an indescribably light and graceful air to the troop, for the feathers waved, nodded, and bended with the wind, and the horses seemed to leave the ground and fly in the air, also.

"They're the first half of what War Lance calls 'the sacred band,'" commented Lessing to the boy.

"Sacred for what?" asked Messenger, in his cold, detached way.

"Sacred for the hell that they raise when it comes to a fight," said Lessing, with more appreciation. "He keeps sixteen bucks around him that he gets out of the cream of the nation. He made some big medicine and discovered with the aid of the chief medicine man of the tribe that if men would attach themselves to him by a special oath, they would get all kinds of Indian blessings."

"Such as what?" said the boy. "And what's the oath?"

"Why, the oath is that once in the band, they'll never leave it. That they'll fight to the death for each other until their chief calls them away from the battle. That they'll charge home in spite of numbers if the call comes, and that they'll never reveal any of the secret councils of the band."

"That's a good deal of an oath," said the boy. "That War Lance can call on any of them to jump off a cliff, then, if he wants to?"

"Of course he can, and they'd do it gladly."

"Well, what are the rewards?"

"Tons of them. While they're on earth, War Lance promises that all the members of the sacred band will be rich, have sons, and stack up coups and scalps until they're the most honored men in the tribe."

"How does he manage that?" asked the boy.

"Well, it's not so hard as you might think. What's Indian riches? Well, hosses, mostly. And about two thirds of the war parties that the sacred band rides on is to lift hosses from the Crows, or somebody else. They run off three hundred, about six months back, right in the middle of winter. As for the rest of the riches, well, the braves that War Lance picks for the band find it pretty easy to get all the wives they want, and a buck with plenty of wives can always have plenty of robes manufactured, and turn 'em into axes, beads, guns, ammunition, and all that, so that his hosses are still in the bank, and growing with interest. And a man with plenty of wives is sure to have some sons. So you see how it works out?"

"Yes, but the scalps and the coups they count so much on?"

"That's the easiest part of all. War Lance keeps those fellows up to the hilt in fighting all the time, and they either count coups and they take scalps, or else they lose their own, pretty pronto. It's easier for them all the time, because they've got such a reputation now that when a bunch of the Crows hears the special war whoop of the band, they take to their heels and run for it. And I don't blame 'em. The sacred band can come up behind on the best hosses that are rode in these here mountains, and they do about as they please. Look at 'em as they come near. There's two ranks in front of War Lance, and two rows behind him."

They came closer. And a wild cheer went up from the watchers.

The sudden shout caused several of the mustangs to try to jump through a hole in the sky, but horse contortions were nothing to those heroes. They sat the animals without a quiver.

"They've got so famous, that band," said Lessing, "that now and then you'll get a famous fighter coming up from another tribe. See that one on the right, that fellow with the heavy shoulders. That's a Cheyenne. He ain't as old as he looks, but he had his face pretty nigh chawed off in a fight with a grizzly. He killed that grizzly and earned the necklace of claws that he's wearing, but you can see that most of his face disappeared durin' the fight. He was a big name in his own tribe, but he come up here to get a little closer to the happy hunting grounds. You see, the sacred band has a special pass to the sky, when it dies."

"A pass to the sky?" echoed Messenger, opening his eyes.

"Certainly. Right up to the sky. The minute that one of them passes in his chips, he's snatched to the happy hunting grounds, and there the Old Man gives him a herd of a hundred hosses, though one hoss would be enough, because they're bred so's they can run all day and never get tired in the fields and the hills of the sky. And then the Old Man walks out a hundred or so beautiful girls, and the hero that's dead, he takes his pick, though there ain't much picking and choosing to do, because each one of them is a little more pretty than the rest, and every one of them is a boss hand at cooking, tanning hides, thinning 'em, making clothes, beading, and all the other kinds of talent that a man would want in a squaw. And up there in the sky grounds, there's billions of buffalo that run like the wind but not so fast as the blue horses."

"Do those fighters believe all of that stuff?" asked the boy, sneering.

"Sure they do, because War Lance has told 'em those things, and he can't be wrong."

"Why not?"

"Because after a man has taken ten scalps and counted twenty coups, he can't tell a lie among the Blackfeet. Likely, War Lance believes all that rot himself. Probably come to him in a dream, and they believe in their dreams more than we believe in our eyes, you can bet."

"They're either half-wits or children never grown up," declared the boy.

"If you get to know 'em better, you'll change your mind," said the trapper. "Look at number three in the first line. That's Sinking Bull, and what's hanging from his bridle reins is three brand-new scalps. They don't look as though they had finished drying out, yet."

The boy shuddered.

"Yeah, it ain't pretty, but you get used to it," said Lessing. "I've taken a couple scalps in my day, myself. One was a Pawnee that tried to count a coup on me before he brained me, and I just managed to run my knife into his gizzard and open him up a mite. I took his hair. Seemed like I needed some kind of a souvenir, that day. Look at them boys go by! Every one of them is ten years younger than he looks, and there ain't a one of them that would trade his place in the sacred band to be President of the United States."

"Murderers, and horse thieves?" said the boy.

But he was stating an opinion, rather than asking a question.

"No, sir!" exclaimed Lessing hotly. "Honorable gentlemen, accordin' to their lights. And there ain't any man that can travel by any light better than the best that he knows about!"

The first two rows went by, sitting proudly, managing their frantic horses as though they hardly knew that the animals were dancing and prancing. Just before the gate there was a shallow ditch, and when the eight leaders reached this place, they reined their horses so that the entire troop vaulted over, bounding high. It was a pretty sight, and they went by Messenger with a whirring of feathers, and a streaming of hair, and a flashing of spear points.

Never had he seen, at close hand, such magnificent specimens of manhood. But, behind the troop, came a horseman and a horse which made the rest vanish even from the cold and calculating brain of the boy.

He started. Instinctively, he put out a hand to grip the arm of his companion.

"Aye, aye," said Lessing. "There's the grandest chief and the hardest fighter in the whole length of the mountains. They're all small birds, compared to that eagle. Look at the head on him, and look at the arms! He's taken more scalps than I ever took bird eggs. That's War Lance, and that's his hoss."

# 9

The eight who had preceded had looked, to the boy, like powerful and graceful predatory animals, in their strength, and in the fierceness and the wildness of their eyes. They did not need fresh scalps dangling from their reins to prove to young Messenger that they were as savage and dangerous as so many tigers. Something swelled up in him, suddenly, hotly.

He himself had been taught all the arts of destruction. He had been prepared through all his life to kill and to avoid death. Those arts he had not practiced. But when he saw these savages, suddenly he was glad with all his heart that his hands had been equipped with uncanny skill.

But though they seemed formidable, there was not one who disturbed his self-confidence in the slightest. Like some champion looking at a group of antagonists, he had measured them calmly, and decided that this man was too heavy for his strength, that one too nervous, yonder fellow too slow. They were the instant judgments which a practiced eye will make in such matters.

Then came War Lance, and it seemed to the boy that the very ground quaked beneath him.

For this was, to be sure, a different matter.

The very horse beneath the chief was different from those which the others bestrode. It was one of those dappled chestnuts, so dark that that dappling, like a faint patterning of leopard spots, was barely distinguishable. Only when the sun struck the velvet of him in a certain way, the design was apparent. He seemed all silk and steel, supple steel that bends and never breaks, sword steel that a warrior can put the trust of his life in. He went with a sober and easy gait. It was only when he looked at the boy that Messenger could tell that the same wild spirit was in him that appeared in all the actions of the other horses. For, in his eyes, a fire flashed from the stallion. It was like the look of a caged eagle, incomparably fierce, and grand, and untamable. One might have said that he submitted to the control of this man because he loved the battle and could endure the matchless valor and strength of his rider.

For so War Lance appeared.

Physically, he seemed the match, and more, for the most powerful of his companions, though they were the picked men of many tribes. As when a thousand athletes walk upon a field, yet one of them, by something in his bearing and the smooth harmony of his might and the carriage of his head, appears a champion, so War Lance appeared among his chosen men.

There was not a touch of paint on the body of the horse or upon the body or the face of the master. In his long hair were set only two eagle feathers.

But those matters of horse and the man's body were purely secondary to Messenger. He looked to the face, and dwelt there, enthralled. The man appeared forty. Being an Indian, he might be perhaps ten years younger. He had the true Indian features. Nose and chin and mouth appeared inflexible in terrible severity, but the brow was nobly made and the eyes were large, luminous, and thoughtful. Perhaps they were a little overbright, like the eyes of the horse he bestrode, but like it, he kept all under perfect control. Suddenly the boy could understand how the braves had listened to the prophecies or the dreams of this man and believed in them.

Here, as the chief came almost opposite, War Lance turned his head, and the bright, keen glance centered suddenly upon the face of Messenger.

It struck Messenger like a blow. It dazzled and dizzied him, and he was blinking and half unnerved when the brass howitzer on top of the fort roared with a deep, hollow reverberation.

He started.

The eight horses which had gone before, at that explosion became frantic and hardly could be restrained by their perfect riders. But not so the stallion and War Lance. With an unaltered step, the great horse came to the edge of the ditch, and seeming merely to stretch out for a slightly longer stride, was somehow across it—an elastic impulse, rather than an actual jump, it seemed to Messenger.

Fierce, keen, overmastering desire and envy suddenly burned in his heart and in his brain.

He had had his training on the best of Kentucky and

Virginia-bred blood horses. On them he had been forced to gallop across the roughest country bareback. On them he had been taught to rise and stand at a gallop. He had had to learn to lay himself along the side of a racing, headlong mount. He had fallen to the ground in every possible posture. His neck had been half broken a hundred times. He had been a mass of bruises and of sores, until that dreadful education was finished. And as his skill had increased, he had been rewarded with still finer and wilder mounts. He had gained a peculiarly savage pleasure in mastering them, one after the other. He had learned to love some of them but never had he seen such a horse as this stallion.

It was a storm-wind incarnate. It was a hurricane gathered in the hand and at the will of the master. Distance did not exist before its stride. Its courage would never fail its strength, and its strength would never fail its courage.

"Yes, sir," said Lessing, at his elbow. "Two looks at that one would turn a saint into a hoss thief, I reckon!"

And he laughed, a little huskily, as though he himself had had the same emotion that burned in the boy.

But that voice, and that laughter, brought young Messenger back to the earth, and he glanced aside at Lessing with something almost like disgust.

Then, however, he could look at the rest of the procession. Rather dimly, he saw the last half of the sacred band go by, and mechanically he told himself that they were a match for the first half of the same troop. Man and beast were as good, perhaps better. But they seemed slight things compared with War Lance and his stallion.

Breathing heavily, as though he had been running up a hill, Messenger surveyed the procession that followed. All the warriors of the tribes which were present at the fort streamed by him. Calmly he told himself that the riders were athletes, nearly every one. Even the old men rode their horses with a wonderful skill.

47

But they meant nothing to Messenger. His heart and his soul were yonder behind the palisades where War Lance was now, perhaps, springing down from his charger.

He turned to Lessing.

"Let's go inside," said he.

"Aye," grinned Lessing. "You wanta have another look at War Lance, close up. But not too close, son. That's the kind of a fire that'll burn you to the heart in a half of a second. Besides, there's something else comin' up here. Doggone me if it don't look like Summer Day has come back here, the skunk! I've told you that I like the Injuns, son, but there's exceptions. And Summer Day is the worst of 'em. The murderin', stealin', faithless, treacherous hound! How come that the Blackfeet and the Piegans would make a chief out of him? Yes, sir, that's Summer Day. I can tell by the way that he hangs his head to one side, like he was sorry for something. And he's got plenty to be sorry for, the scoundrel! That's Summer Day, and dang lot of insolence he's got to come back here to the fort!"

"Who is he?" asked the boy, hardly hearing his own question, so disturbed was his mind by other thoughts.

"Why," said Lessing, "he's the real head chief of the Blackfeet. War Lance has got more fame for fightin', but Summer Day is a good second to him. And besides, Summer Day is a grand, high-flyin' medicine man of the first water. He can wither your face in a night, and bend your back double in a day, the Injuns believe. He gets rich curin' fools. Hot baths is his main hold, like it is with all of 'em, but his lingo is better than most, and they believe in him. Besides, he's got a terrible long list of scalps and coups, and more hosses than anybody else in the whole nation. Yes, sir, that's old Summer Day. Not old, either, except in meanness. He killed a half-breed at the fort here, right after it was opened, and then he faded out into the open

48

country. What's brought him back—unless War Lance done some persuadin'!"

This chief had chosen, oddly enough, to take the absolutely rearmost position in the line of warriors, and behind him began the rout of children and women who poured behind, but leaving a safe distance of respect and fear between them and the great medicine man. He was a beast of a man. His hair was like that of a horse's tail—as long and as coarse, and some of it tumbled unheeded down across his face. A monster of a man, in his sleekly sloping shoulders appeared the immeasurable power of an animal. He did not have a picture horse, like one of the sacred band. Instead, he rode a shaggy, typical pony, though doubtless it possessed hidden virtues. As he came by, the chief lifted his eyes, and glanced with a glittering look to the side.

Messenger stood stiff as a lance.

"It is he!" he gasped.

And Lessing, turning suddenly upon him, amazed, saw that the boy was as white as stone, and knew that he had found the object of his quest.

The inclosure within the palisade was now swarming with mounted men, women, and children, and the dust began to rise like smoke around the fort, while Lessing still remained outside the wall, gazing at his companion.

"You want that scalp, son?" he said to Messenger. "You want to get at Summer Day, do you?"

Messenger continued to stare wildly in the direction in which the enemy had disappeared.

"I have to have him," he said. "I need him more than I need air to breathe. I have to have him! That would make me a free man!"

The trapper shook his head in astonishment.

"You might as well," said he, "try to take the scalp of the thunderbird. You might better try to take the scalp of War Lance himself!"

The boy looked at him with the same burning glance. He looked like one in a frenzy.

"Tell me why?" said he.

"Because," declared the trapper, "War Lance is a great fighter, and he has sixteen chosen men behind him, but Summer Day is really the most powerful man in the tribe. He's the one who mixes up the victory medicine for 'em. He's the one that they carry presents to. You could hit at War Lance through sixteen braves. You'd have to hit at Summer Day through the whole Blackfoot nation. I tell you what, even if you got at him, he's a terror. I'd hate to be locked up in a room with him. Even if I had four fightin' men with me. He'd be wearin' our hair before the finish of the fight, I tell you! Try anything that you want, Messenger. Try War Lance, even, but don't go throwin' yourself away on a job like the medicine man!"

Messenger made an abrupt gesture.

"Let's see what's up," said he, and he led the way through the gate into the big inclosure.

They got, eventually, to fairly good places for observation of what followed, for the crowd of people were stirring so restlessly that it was not hard to drift a way through them. Louis Desparr had come down from the roof, and now he stood in the entrance to the store with a pipe in his hand

and a broad smile on his face. This visit from so great a man as War Lance, to say nothing of the head medicine man among the Blackfeet, assured his future prosperity, he felt. And he could not help exhibiting some of his joy.

War Lance and Summer Day, in the meantime, pressing up to the lead of the warriors, with a few motions drove them back until a circle was cleared. Then, dismounting, the two chiefs approached the trader. Their greetings were dignified, though rather cold. Now that the two famous Blackfeet were side by side, the contrast between them was more startling than in the line of march. The high head and the magnificent carriage of War Lance were opposed to the cunning and downward look of the medicine man, who appeared to be swallowing a smile and brooding upon mischief beyond the fathoming of ordinary men. Yet he appeared in his own way as formidable an enemy as the great war chief himself. All that trickery and foxlike cunning could do were implied in the presence of Summer Day.

War Lance made a speech, at once. He spoke briefly and simply. This voice was like a deep and mellow thunder, reassuring, but filling the hearers with awe.

He said in the Blackfoot tongue: "My friend, several moons ago, the great medicine man of the Blackfeet came to this place and killed a man. Then he went away quickly. He did not run away because he was afraid, but because he felt that he might have been wrong, and he did not want to start a fight between all his people and the white men. When I heard of this, I went to him and asked him if it would not be a good thing if he would come back and make that killing right. The man he killed had a value and a price. Summer Day has come back to find out what the price may be, and then he will pay it, and the Blackfeet will be friends forever with the white men."

He paused, and Summer Day with a single gesture signified his assent.

51

Louis Desparr nodded at them in the most friendly way.

"This is the way honest people ought to act," he declared. "I cannot say what the value of Henry Adams was. But his widow is still here. There she stands, now."

Mrs. Adams was a full-blooded Cree, and not the most beautiful of her race. She was a burly creature, with shoulders like a man, and long, hanging arms.

"Here is Summer Day come back like a good man to pay you for your dead husband," said Desparr. "What price do you want to put? You name a price, and let Summer Day name one. I'll see which comes nearest to being honest."

Mrs. Adams raised her long arms to the sky and let out a wail, as the beginning of her price-setting.

"Listen!" said Lessing at the ear of Messenger. "She'll want a whole herd of hossflesh for that worthless half-breed of hers."

Mrs. Adams at last reduced her keening to a voice that could be understood and announced that her tepee was desolate, and her children were hungry, and the hunter was gone from her side, and alone and sadly she faced life, which promised to be always winter. She wound up by saying that fifty horses would be about right, but she added that a couple of good axes and a few pounds of beads ought to be thrown in to restore good will perfectly on all sides.

"You've heard the woman," said Desparr to Summer Day. "Now, what price do you put on the head of the man you killed?"

Summer Day hardly lifted his head to answer, and when he spoke he looked neither at Desparr nor at the squaw, but across the palisade toward the distant hills and the blue mist of mountains. It was as though he found these foolish conferences with ordinary men almost too dull to be worth his speech.

Finally he said: "That man was neither white nor red. He was neither weak enough to lie down, nor strong enough to

52

stand up. He was nothing. Besides, he stole from me, or tried to steal. But to make this woman happy, and not because I did wrong, I will give her two horses. That is enough to give for such a man!"

"That Summer Day," observed Lessing, "would get fat on thistles, I tell you. Listen to him, will you?"

"Aye," said Messenger grimly. "I'm listening to him!"

The squaw, in the meantime, broke into a fresh clamor, but Desparr silenced her with a few words.

"You know," he said, "that your husband was a lazy man. He never killed a buffalo in his life, and the only elk meat you ever ate was given to you here in the fort, or by your friends in your tribe. He would not hunt like an Indian, and he would not work like a white man. Now, then, fifty horses are a great deal too much to ask for him. You know that you have a good, warm home here, as long as you choose to work and behave. Your children are being taken care of twice as well as they were when your husband was alive. Eight horses are enough to pay, if Summer Day will give that many!"

At this judgment, or attempt at one, the woman screamed out as though she had been stabbed to the heart.

Her babel of noise lasted until she saw the hand of the medicine man raised. No matter what her excitement, the awe with which he filled all around him was easily to be observed. Her voice gradually died into a doglike whining, while Summer Day said: "You can have five horses. That is enough. Two horses are too much. But I am generous. I give you three more, because you are a foolish woman, and fools need to have plenty of wealth."

She screeched again. She began to roll her eyes and a great piercing lament for the dead Henry Adams went up to the sky.

Suddenly the medicine man struck his hands together, and as the palms joined, there was a loud exclamation and a general shrinking back by all who stood around, while the widow was turned to stone. For a brilliant play of blue fire had spurted out as the hands struck home, like the splashing of heavily struck water.

Then Summer Day exclaimed in a harsh voice: "You are wicked and of no worth. Five horses you will take, at once, or get none at all. Do you think that I do not see you and your whole life? You are not sorry that you have lost a husband. You are glad, and already you have found another man!"

This revelation, for the truth of it she did not contest, made poor Mrs. Adams utterly dumb. She no longer resisted, but nodded her head mutely when the trader asked her if this settlement was satisfactory.

In the meantime, two or three boys left the inclosure and came back driving before them five little typical Indian ponies, with rather lumpish heads and shaggy coats.

The awe which had been inspired in the breast of Mrs. Adams by the bit of parlor magic, and the apparent prophetic insight of the chief, were now diminished a little by her disappointment. And she asked some of the bystanders if these really were horses or simply big dogs which would eat her out of house and home. However, she took the five very gladly by the rawhide lariats which were fastened to their necks, and so she led them away, and the affair of the murdered Henry Adams was concluded.

This Louis Desparr, speaking in the Indian tongue, said: "Now here this trouble is ended. The woman has been paid. She has taken the price. She will forget that she had a husband. If there is any more hard talk about the death of Adams, then I will be the enemy of the men who quarrel. So will all good men."

Here Summer Day put in a word for himself.

With his unpleasantly secret smile and eye turned off toward the horizon again, he said: "I have shown you that I am a good man. I have paid the woman. If there is any man who has a claim against me, let me hear him speak."

He turned his head slowly around the circle until his eyes rested upon the face of Messenger.

"I am here to make a claim!" said the boy.

# 11

The calm and superior smile of the medicine man went out like a torch struck by wind and rain. He looked at the young man and he looked again.

And, from the Indians who were pressing closer and closer, there went up a sharp, excited babbling—instantly followed by deep silence, as all ears strained to catch the words. For though Messenger spoke in the Blackfoot tongue, his voice was pitched so low that those at any distance found it hard to make out what he was saying.

The interruption of the ceremony of the reconciliation, which ought to have called for a feast on the spot, caused War Lance to turn sharply about, also, and to stare at Messenger.

The medicine man did not deign to answer the stranger directly. Instead, he gestured to some who stood near.

"Tell this white boy who I am," said he. "And ask him what he can want from me. Perhaps he wants a horse to ride? Tell him that I never refuse beggars!"

He had said this loudly enough for the white man to hear, however, and young Messenger replied, using the same tactics of addressing the nearest people and not the magic-worker directly: "I hear that this is the great wonder-worker, the medicine man of all the Blackfeet, the famous Summer Day?"

"Yes!" burst out a chorus of voices.

Summer Day allowed the smile of scorn to return to his features.

"I hear," went on Messenger, "that Summer Day can call the spirits out of the sky so that they chatter to him through the smoke hole of his tepee."

"We have heard the voices!" exclaimed the crowd.

The content of the medicine man grew greater and greater. It appeared as though the white man had come there to praise their great chief of the Blackfeet, not to make any real demand upon him. Only War Lance, standing somewhat apart, continued to look in fixed thought at the white boy.

"He can," resumed Messenger in his recital, "he can take away the life of people who are a long way off."

"Yes. He has done it many times!"

"He can bring back to life people whose spirits are already in the happy hunting grounds, and ready to leap on the backs of the blue sky-horses."

A perfect shout of confirmation answered him.

"Then," said the white boy, "what I am asking him to do will not be too hard. I am asking him to give back the life of a white man he murdered."

All Indian smiles disappeared suddenly, though War Lance was seen to nod a little to himself, almost as though he had been expecting some such announcement as made the climax of this speech of apparent praise.

As for the medicine man, his ugly face had a glint of evil malice.

"I have taken many scalps," he declared. "The Blackfeet know it."

"Yes, yes!" they replied, hurriedly, their eyes fixed upon the face of the white boy who dared to say so much before the dreadful favorite of the spirits!

"I have taken many scalps of Indians, and many of white warriors, too," said the medicine man calmly. "Which one do you mean?"

"Look back a good many years, to a time when you were a very young man, Summer Day. You were not quite so famous then, but you were already a great medicine man and liar."

Summer Day started with a convulsive fury, but this he controlled instantly.

"Very well," said he. "You have called me a liar. I am able to listen before I act. The spirits listen, also. I think that I hear them laughing above my head!"

He pointed solemnly into the air.

"In that time, a good many great suns ago," went on the boy, "you once went through the woods and came on a white man in a small camp. He was all alone. He had broken his leg and was lying there trying to get well. His friend who was taking care of him had left camp to go hunting. Now do you remember, Summer Day?"

The medicine man actually smiled again, there was such a demon in him!

"I remember the killing of many white men," he said insolently. "But this one is not in my mind."

"You will remember," said the boy, in his usual calm manner. "You will remember that you asked the helpless white man where his friend had gone and when he would be back, and when the white man would not tell, you tortured him. You pushed splinters into his body and lighted them and let them burn into the flesh. You twisted a cord around his head and tightened it until it cut to the bone and almost forced the eyes out of his head. You cut the tendons of his arms and legs one by one. But still he would not betray his friend. At last, you brained him with his own camp ax, and you took his scalp. Do you remember these things now, brave chief?"

The assurance with which the boy talked had its own effect, and the medicine man, looking suddenly around him, could not help realizing that the picture was not a pretty one. Torture had its own place in the Indian scheme of things. But it was rather a religious rite than a thing for personal indulgence. After the great battle, when many of the braves of the nation had fallen, it was then of some account to pacify the spirits of the dead by sending some of their recent enemies to a death by torment. But it was a thing to be done by ecstasy and not soberly in ordinary fighting. The sleeping or the helpless had no right of life, to be sure, but this picture, deliberately drawn, of the badgering of a man who could not strike back, made even the toughest of the Blackfoot warriors wrinkle their faces in disgust.

The medicine man, when he saw that his case was not a desirable one, merely sneered as he looked away toward the hills in the distance.

"We hear many men talk," said he, "but how often do we hear the truth? Truth is like a very fleet deer. It runs away when the white men come near. What has made this young boy think that I, chief among the Blackfeet, have done such a thing?"

"First of all," said Messenger, "I could have guessed it by the beast in your face. But secondly, I had something that was a surer proof. You had tormented the poor white man until his brain was sick. You had blinded him in one eye. You had slashed his left arm and both his legs so that he had only one thing that he could move, and that was his right hand.

"Then you left him lying there, while you went off about the camp to see what would be worth stealing. You did not want to kill him in a hurry, but you wanted him to taste his agony as long as possible. Finally, you came back to finish him, but in the meantime, he had done a thing which you could not suspect.

"You have your painters and your artists, Summer Day. They can draw a buffalo very well. They can even draw a horse, so that the horse can be recognized. Well, that white man had spent his life making drawings and paintings. Whatever he saw with his eyes, he could make the face of it with his hands. And when you went off to plunder the camp, he found at his side on the ground a broad, fresh, white chip of wood that you had newly slashed from a log to try the edge of the ax. When he saw the chip, it must have made the white man think of clean, fresh paper. He had for a pencil the tip of his finger. He had for paint his own red blood. On the chip, then, he drew the face of the Indian who had murdered him, and under it he scrawled one word: '*Blackfoot!*' Very well, now you shall see the face that he drew!"

The crowd, hardly breathing during this recital, now muttered one to another as Messenger took from an inside pocket a strong wallet. He opened and took from within it a flat package wrapped securely in silk. This he undid with the greatest care.

As he worked, he went on gravely and almost gently: "As the chip grew older and dried, it became less white. It bent. And finally it cracked in two. However, it can still be put together, and the picture can be recognized, I think."

With this, he put the silk into his pocket, and fixing the two halves of the chip together, he raised into the air, with both hands, that extraordinary picture, and turned slowly around to let all about him observe the thing.

It was no more than three inches wide and perhaps five or six in length. The red blood of the pigment that had been used for paint long ago had blackened with time. The strokes were in themselves very gross and heavy, for a fingertip could not be expected to make delicate lines. But as an expert worker with charcoal will rough in the most striking likeness, so that tortured and dying man had worked with his own blood and with his finger, subduing his pain, making his brain clear while he sketched.

Underneath it was clumsily written, as though with a failing strength, the word "Blackfoot." But that word was not needed, now. The face was enough. Rough as the work was, the likeness was there. The straggling of the hair across the face, the forward and sidewise cant of the head would in themselves have been almost enough; but, in addition, the leering smile appeared there, and even, as it seemed to the excited watchers, the brilliant, brutal eyes of the medicine man staring out from beneath his straggling forelocks.

So great and startling was the likeness, and so much had even the toughest of the braves been worked up by the scene that went before the showing of the picture, that as the boy finished turning, the pent emotions burst out in one deep and general exclamation from children, women, and men.

"Summer Day!"

The boy returned the chip carefully to its wrapping of silk and replaced it in his wallet. As he put this into the pocket from which it had been taken, he said:

"Now, Summer Day, tell these people that you've been a liar as well as a murderer!"

# 12

An old fox is hard to corner.

Summer Day, even now, failed to look at his accuser. Even now he maintained his smile, and his distant look toward the horizon. Then he raised his hand.

"The spirits!" he said. "The spirits which told me to kill that man, they are with me now. They are just over my head. They are laughing, and glad that I have done what I have done. Yes, my friends, and the good scalp still hangs in my tepee. My wives admire it. The hair still shines like gold. They brush the soot from the smoke out of it. They say that it looks like the white man's money. I killed that man, I remember now. I counted three coups on him."

There was a single murmur. It came from the throat of War Lance, but there was no speech in the sound. It was simply a deep-voiced note of disapproval, and it was echoed, a moment later, by a sort of groan that passed through all the throng.

At this, Summer Day actually put back his head and laughed. He turned a bit, and his odd, shifting glances went over the faces.

"You think I have done wrong?" he exclaimed. "Is there a man of you who ever has seen or talked to spirits, except the ones I have sent to you? Why do you frown at me? I am only two hands for the Sky People to use, two ears with which they hear, two eyes with which they see and—remember!"

This last cunningly implied threat had such a force that Messenger, who was watching all things and faces like a hawk, actually saw the bravest and the greatest of those warriors drop their heads a little—even War Lance half turned away, shaking his head, apparently baffled by disgust and yet controlled by the awe with which the chief medicine man always fills a tribe.

Summer Day had struck a subtle but a telling blow, and now he could afford to pay direct attention to the young white man.

"Now this boy comes to talk to me," said the chief. "Perhaps he wants more horses, also? Well, I have plenty of them in my herd. Let somebody ask him how many horses he would like to have. I still have horses—for beggars!"

And, behind the boy, the voice of the trapper said almost in the ear of Messenger: "Take the horses. That's honorable. That will keep your dignity, in the eyes of the braves. Don't you worry about that."

"I don't worry about that," the boy assured him.

Then, staring fixedly at the medicine man, he raised his arm and pointed toward the green, rolling lands beyond the gate and the palisade.

"There is plenty of room there," he said. "What I want to say to you about that murder, I would like to say out there. And anybody who wants to, can watch my words!"

He had caught the true Indian idiom and their manner of talk. And the idea of "watching" words tickled the Blackfoot fancy so intensely that there was a stir among the warriors and a sudden flashing of light across their faces.

As for the medicine man, he now brought his glance back from the horizon, at which he had been sneering and smiling for so long. He allowed that glance to rest burningly upon the face of the boy, before he said: "This is a young man. Someone should tell him who I am. Or perhaps he will have one or two friends who will go along with him to fight me?"

This supreme self-confidence was not surprising to the Blackfeet. There were no three of them, with the possible exception of War Lance, who would have dared to confront the miracle man in any sort of a battle.

But young Messenger tipped back his head a little and laughed. It was not forced laughter. It flowed out with a clear, sharp, ringing sound that made one think of the chiming of the cold waters of the mountain streams.

"Summer Day, Summer Day," he cried out, "you are about to die! I am going to kill you, and that will make me a free man. Shall I give you a sign of your death?"

The medicine man kept his face fairly well, though in the presence of this easy laughter, and this taunting, confident speech it was not easy to do.

He waited for an instant, as his wrath gathered, and into that moment of pause dropped the cawing of a crow, which was wheeling above the yard of the fort.

"I shall give you a sign of your own death!" exclaimed the worker of wonders, the fire-dealer.

"I shall kill you with fires from the sky!" he shouted, losing his calm like a robe and standing in unconcealed rage before the crowd. "I shall kill you with the blue fires of the sky!"

And, striking his hands above his head, once more, before the eyes of all men, blue flames were seen to spurt out from between them. There was literally a groan of awe. Even War Lance, striding back half a step, had to brace himself to endure the sight of this miracle.

The heart of the medicine man was comforted, but only for a moment. Then he heard Messenger laughing again.

"That's your sign, and a very poor sign," said the boy. "That's a trick which half a dozen cheap little hired medicine men do every day among the whites. But here's a sign that's worth ten of that. Look over your heads!"

Every eye suddenly glanced up, as though they expected that the sky itself might be opening.

They saw there the heavy-winged crow, which had jumped itself half a dozen yards higher in the air, at the gesture and the shout of Summer Day, and since they stared earnestly, expecting some sort of a great thing to happen, only two or three of those nearest to the boy saw his hand flash up, with a gun in it. The others merely heard the revolver explode and saw the crow, high above them, tip suddenly over to the side, stagger, and then slide slanting downward towards the ground. It tumbled head over heels, and landed on the ground with a thump which was audible in the dead silence that followed the report of the weapon.

This was no miracle. It was simply a case of snap shooting that made the eyes start in their heads.

They began to mumble and mutter.

No matter how extremely clever the magic of the medicine man might be, this outright exposure of shooting skill was enough to make them all shake their heads. Certainly it wiped the sneer off the face of the chief. And in the eyes of War Lance appeared suddenly a glint of hope and pleasure which barely glimmered there and was gone again.

Said War Lance solemnly: "This young man has asked you to go out and fight with him, Summer Day. He is a rash young man, but he does not seem afraid. He is standing there and waiting for your answer."

Summer Day favored the speaker with a sudden, dark glance, but then he smoothed his expression again.

He pointed, in his turn, through the open gate of the fort and across the green plain.

"Do you see, my friends," said he, "where the river makes the bend, and where it cuts away half the hill and leaves the high red bank?"

They could see. It was the plainest landmark in sight.

The narrow, swift river, leaving the hills, here leaped out into the plain with a snowy face covered with froth. On the right of its mouth there stood a round-headed hill, the top of which was covered with a tall growth of trees, and darkened with shrubs toward the edges.

"There is Thunder Hill," said the medicine man. "Go out and ride into it from the left, I shall ride into it from the right. At the top of the mountain I shall meet you and pull down the blue fires and the red fires out of the sky to burn you."

"Don't take that challenge," said the old trapper, anxious at the back of the boy. "You must not take that challenge!"

"Why not?"

"You know guns. You may know hosses, boxing, wrestling, and all of that. You may climb trees like a cat, but you don't know hunting. And Summer Day does. He's one of the greatest stalkers that ever pulled the whiskers out of a mountain lion and cut his throat when he woke up. Don't be a fool, boy!"

Young Messenger made no reply; there was too much truth in what Lessing said for him to turn the advice aside at once.

And the trapper went on: "You most likely could shoot the eyes out of his head, in an open fight, and he knows it! But in there among the trees, it'll be the best stalker that wins. Mind that, Messenger!"

But here the loud, taunting voice of the medicine man broke in: "What does the young man answer? If his heart is growing cold, let him go away. I have already so many white scalps, what does one more mean to me?"

"Summer Day," said the boy through his teeth, "I offered to fight you in the open. But if you prefer the dark, I'll meet you there. Perhaps it's as well that no one should see what I intend to do to you!"

# 13

Not for a moment did Lessing leave the side of his protégé and he poured out good advice to him constantly.

"Messenger," he asked, "tell me—you never hunted so much as a squirrel?"

"No."

As he talked briefly, Messenger was looking over his weapons. He lacked a horse, and Lessing had sent a boy to saddle his own pony. The Colt revolver had to be cleaned and reloaded in all its chambers, to make sure that it was in the most perfect working order. And, in the meantime, they stood aside from the crowd, close to the palisade. The medicine man, also, had withdrawn with a circle of companions, behind the shelter of whom he was donning his war paint, and looking to his own fighting tools.

"You've never been out in the wilderness?" asked the trapper, with more and more anxiety.

"No, never before this trip."

"You don't know how to walk over dry leaves, and over twigs?"

"No."

"Then fetch off those boots and put on these moccasins. They're old, and that makes them all the better. They ain't got soles, and that means that they'll let you feel the ground with the palm of your foot like the palm of your hand. Look where you step, but keep feeling the ground like you were feeling for diamonds. Put your foot down, toe first and the roll forward on it—like this."

Messenger, without a word, pulled off his boots and put on the moccasins, as directed.

As he stood up again, the trapper continued: "Them that get into the woods where there's trouble ahead of 'em make the mistake of glancin' around too many times. That ain't the way. Notice a deer or a wild cat when it's out in danger. It don't jerk its head around. It gives a good long look at anything that's interesting. Give them same long looks. Sink your eye right down into the green of the branches and maybe you'll find something that's worthwhile. Keep markin' the things that are around you. A tree that you can jump behind—a log that you can drop behind—a bunch of brush that would shelter a growed-up man. And always remember that an Injun knows how to fade himself out into the grass and make himself as small as a snake, because they got a lot of snake in their natures. And an Injun can hide all of himself behind a sapling that would hide a white baby, two year old. Remember them things. Get yourself on a hairtrigger—and heaven help you!"

Messenger, suddenly, as the horse was brought up, held out his hand.

"You're a friend, Lessing," said he.

The trapper shook the extended hand with warmth.

"If I had a week in the woods with you," he said, "I could teach you something worthwhile. But even then, I couldn't teach you what the Injuns are born knowing."

"If he gets me," said the boy, "he'll probably take the

horse that I've ridden on up to the edge of the woods. If he does, it'll be your loss. Here's my wallet. You'll find enough cash in that to make up to you for the loss of the horse and the saddle—"

"I don't want your money, son."

"You don't want it, but you'd better keep it for me."

"I won't touch it. It'd bring you bad luck. If there's any message that you'd like to send out by me—"

The youngster raised his head and looked thoroughly straight before him.

"No," he said at last. "There's no message. Those who are interested, they'll hear about the end of me, in time. Goodbye, Lessing!"

He shook hands once more, and turning, he suddenly leaped into the saddle.

Lessing's pinto, a tough little bronco with the look of an overwise speculator, greeted the stranger with a leap straight into the air, scattering those who stood curiously nearby. As they fell back, shouting in alarm, they saw the moccasined feet of the lad find the stirrups as if by instinct, and as the pony landed, its ribs were in such a crushing grip that it decided straightway that it had met its master. And off it jogged through the gate of the Lippewan Fort as though it expected to have a long journey before it. Summer Day, on his long-haired war pony, followed a moment later.

He was stripped to the waist. His face and body were fairly glistening with war paint. Now, prepared for battle, and with his body erect in the saddle, he looked far closer to the beau ideal of the perfect warrior. And as he went out from among the Blackfeet, they gave him a rousing cheer.

They had been moved by the tale of the white lad, and the sight of the picture painted in blood, but now their sympathies were strongly drawn back to the side of their champion who was to represent them against the white man.

The eyes of the red men shone with excitement, and, mounting their horses, they streamed out over the grassy plain and the rolling hills to come as close as possible to the place of the encounter. The people of the fort left it, also, Louis Desparr riding at the side of his friend, Lessing, while the two champions, diverging to the right and the left, came up to the opposite sides of the hill, as had been planned.

There, on the verge of the green gloom of the woods which covered the height, Messenger drew rein and dismounted. His rifle he was about to take with him, but on second thought he abandoned it.

In that dense forest, it was highly unlikely that he would have a chance to shoot at a greater distance than that which his revolver covered with accuracy.

He looked back at the hills beneath. There were still a few stragglers coming out from the fort, dashing their horses forward at full speed; and the fort itself looked small and dark, against the silver flash of the river that almost surrounded it. Nearer at hand, in a long, loose semicircle, were gathered every man, woman, and child of the tribes who were present at Fort Lippewan. They were watching, no doubt, with their hearts in their mouths.

And he himself?

There was an odd chill in the pit of his stomach, and a feeling of lightness in his brain, which he knew was fear. But he merely smiled at it. Life, after all, had not been a thing so sweet to him that he should make any desperate effort to retain the spark of it. He could not help shuddering when he thought of the mutilation which would befall him if the medicine man should win the battle. He shuddered still more at his mental picture of Summer Day galloping his horse down into the plain with the triumphant screech of the war cry bursting from his throat, and the new scalp, dangling from his bridle rein.

Then he put these pictures resolutely behind him, and entered the forest.

He had made up his mind on the way to the scene of the battle. No matter what the advice of the old trapper, he could not expect to match the woodcraft of the Indian.

Therefore, he charged almost blindly for the center of the battlefield. That is to say, he ran straight up the slope of the mountain until he came to the crest of the hill.

It was very broad, and the growth of trees, here, was fairly open, far more so than had been the case along the lower slopes. There were plenty of hiding places and stalking places, however. There were clumps of shrubbery and there were nests of rock, also, outcropping here and there.

In the maze of possibilities, it was almost beyond doubt that the Indian would have the best of him. He could not expect to outwit that natural hunter.

For that reason, he had hurried up to the crest. It was hardly likely that the cunning Blackfoot would follow the same tactics, and, therefore, he probably had a moment or two in which to prepare for the encounter.

He picked out for the purpose a good, stout tree which grew a little east of the summit, though almost upon the same level. To this he went, and as he approached, he studied the branches with a good deal of care.

They were by no means as thick as he had hoped to find them, and the foliage was not impenetrable to the eye. Yet at least the upper limbs were fairly well lost in the green mist of the leaves.

He decided, after a glance around, that he could hardly do better with the means at hand, so up the trunk he went, catlike, sure of hand and foot.

He was glad of the light gear on his feet, now. It made the grip of his feet almost as secure as that of his hands. And so he went upward swiftly to a fork well toward the upper middle of the tree. There he stretched himself out along the fork and the branch beneath it, and waited.

# 14

He was facing, now, the trail which he himself had made coming up the hill. Through the spray of the branches and the leaves, he could keep a fairly good lookout on the lower slope, and his hope was simply that the clever Indian would find the trail and, coming up it, expose himself to the fire of the revolver. He did not ask for more than one fair glimpse of Summer Day. A .44 caliber slug would tell the rest of the story, so far as Summer Day was concerned.

There were other chances that might tell against him. Situated as he was, he could not easily turn and look behind him. However, by moving his head up and down and to the right, he could command all the landmarks which he had passed during the last of his journey up the hill, and if the Indian came up along the trail, it would go hard if the boy did not see him.

The branch was not the most comfortable resting place in the world. The hard, narrow round of it bit into his body, but he was long used to discomforts and he endured this with the calm of a Spartan, and maintained his watch.

The minutes went on very slowly.

What amazed him, at first, was the utter silence. But after a time, this was altered. The sound of his own breathing, and the beating of his own heart, after the run and the climb, to say nothing of mental excitement, had served as a blanket to muffle the noises which, as he presently perceived, filled the air. Above all there was a soft, dull, droning sound, which he now made out to be the booming of the river between its hollow banks.

The leaves, too, were not entirely motionless, not entirely silent, but they kept up, here and there, hushing sounds of secrecy. Next, in a pine tree, he saw a squirrel, which ran out on a branch and chattered with amazing loudness at something on the ground. He craned his neck to see what this could be, but he distinguished nothing.

A moment later, a hawk flew over the wood, skimming the tops of the trees. He uttered a scream that sounded hoarse and distant, though the bird was at the time only a few rods away. Then it disappeared beyond the treetops. Next, a blue jay flew like the streak of a dazzling jewel in motion across the clearing just before him.

It whirled up into the air. It hung above his treetop, and uttered a harsh cry. And still it hung about that tree, flashing its gaudy body in the sun, so near that he distinctly heard the whirring of its wings.

And this, if he had known enough of woodland creatures and their ways and what these tell to the observant, would have worried him, or actually driven him out of the tree.

Long moments still dragged slowly by, and then he had sight of his quarry.

It came suddenly. Clearly in view, Summer Day stepped out of the covert of a group of saplings, standing closely, shoulder to shoulder, and with his body drooped forward toward the ground, he made long, silent strides for the next cover.

The heart of the boy leaped. He leveled his revolver—and then found his finger still and unwilling upon the trigger!

He had thought that, being committed to the ways and the tricks of Indian warfare for this combat, he could fight as the Indians fight, subtly, secretly, without mercy when an advantage fell into his hands.

But his heart spoke in him, and he could not fire. The next instant, the form was gone!

At this, he gritted his teeth and told himself that he was a fool. But it hardly mattered, for the man was sure to steal closer and show himself for a surer shot.

Here the blue jay swerved again above his tree, circling, and uttered his cry. But this the boy paid no heed to.

There was something else to occupy him, and freeze his mind with attention.

He stared at a nest of rocks, from behind which the skulking form of Summer Day was sure to step the next instant.

But Summer Day was apparently taking his time!

The minutes went by. No Indian appeared. A vague restlessness and doubt came to the boy. He began to look hastily from side to side, until he remembered what the trapper had told him.

Hasty glances are worth very little in the thick of the wood. A long and penetrating stare is the proper thing. So he began to use the lesson, carefully, as one who knows how to follow instructions. Still he could not pierce the screen of the foliage, or of the trunks, and the scattering rocks.

Then something flew crackling, snapping, through the branches, cutting off a twig an inch from his nose, and the ringing report of a rifle clanged in his ear!

He looked to the right and down.

There was just the hint of the gleam of steel beside the

trunk of a great tree, and he knew what it meant.

Somehow, the Indian had received a warning in time, and circling the tree in which Messenger had his covert, he had had his chance to draw a careful bead, and to fire! What could have made him miss, at such pointblank range unless, making deadly sure, he had insisted on a head shot, and some slight movement of the green branches had diverted his aim?

Those wonderings and that observance took a fifth part of a second for the boy. In the next instant he was off that branch, and swinging by his hands.

And, as he looked down, he saw that Summer Day had dropped his rifle and was running forward.

It was too late to change his own plan, but easy enough to see the wile of the medicine man. He would not waste time in trying to reload his gun. Instead, he would rush out, and as the white lad dropped to the ground, spring on him with his knife.

Already it was prepared in his hand, a long curve of glistening steel. That very knife, perhaps, might have been used to torture the helpless man those years ago!

Releasing his hold on the bending bough, Messenger shot down. He held the revolver straight above him with his right hand. With his left, he caught strongly at bunches of twigs and at small boughs, and these brief handholds, broken almost as fast as they were made, slowed up the force of the fall so that he descended with a heavy shock, to be sure, but on his feet!

And Summer Day, as he lunged in, found himself looking into the eye of a leveled revolver.

He was no coward, however. The same wild spirit which is in every true red warrior was in him, and with a screech of frantic battle exultation, he flung himself at Messenger.

Twice, the latter, in that final instant, pressed the trigger, and twice he could not shoot down a man unequally armed.

Finally, with a groan, he struck at the armed hand of Summer Day with the barrel of the heavy weapon.

Right across the knife blade, held rigidly forward, the blow fell, and with a tinkling sound like that of broken glass, the knife blade snapped.

It was almost too late, but the medicine man sensed instantly what had happened, and bounded to the side.

The useless hilt he still grasped in his convulsed hand, and with his legs planted wide apart and his body stooped forward, he confronted the white man with no surrender in his bearing.

It was the end, however.

He knew what real magic lay in the revolver which Messenger carried. He himself had neither revolver nor even pistol to fall back upon, now. He had his bare hands, and the useless knife hilt. It would give weight to a blow, but it could not parry a flying bullet.

And Messenger smiled as he looked on the medicine man.

The latter, frenzied by the knowledge of his helplessness, actually stamped upon the ground, and a thin bubbling foam formed on his lips.

"Now, Summer Day," said Messenger, "the time has come for you! You are no more, now, than a twig in my hand. I can break you when I please. Do you understand?"

Great shudders passed through the body of the other. But suddenly he drew himself up. The battle mask dropped from his features. He cast the worthless knife hilt behind him.

"My friend," said he, "what you say is true. Summer Day is no more than a child before you, so long as that gun is in your hands. But you will see. The spirits still help me. They will not let me fall before a bullet!"

# 15

To Messenger there came a desperate and deep satisfaction. He now had accomplished his work. The end of the long trail was at hand. A touch of the trigger made him a free man in every sense of the word.

These thoughts, streaming through his mind, almost obscured the words which the medicine man had spoken to him, but he was able to smile coldly, and say: "Tell me, Summer Day, what will your spirits do to help you? How will they turn aside the bullet which I am about to shoot into your brain?"

"How can I tell?" said the medicine man. "Am I one to read every thought of the Sky People? No, now and then, when I pray, they reveal themselves and the future to me. Who am I to command and direct them? Their thoughts and their ways are better than anything that I could invent."

The white man smiled again. "You talk very well, Summer Day," said he. "But I don't think that you have anything that will outweigh the bullet inside of this gun."

"The bullet," said the medicine man calmly, "will never be fired."

"Ah? Never fired?" said Messenger, tightening his grip a little upon the handle of the Colt.

"No, for you will not do a murder, my friend of the iron hand."

"Murder?" cried the white man through his teeth. "You detestable scoundrel, what was it that you did when you found the helpless white man in his camp and killed him slowly?"

"Look!" said the Indian, and pointed over his head.

Messenger was not foolish enough to be tempted into an unwary gesture. But he could still look up and keep the Indian somewhat vaguely within the range of his vision. So up he stared, and he saw before him a small bird flying hastily across the blue of the sky and, above it, a hawk stooping with folded wings.

Down at the little bird the hawk dropped, but as the quarry shifted, footing lightly to the side, the hawk missed his stroke and plunged sheer down for a hundred yards or so past his mark. Then his wings exploded, and the force of his downward drop caused him to jump up again into the blue almost to his former height of place. Again he dropped, and again. Each time he missed, but the fugitive was forced to descend closer and closer to the earth, instead of circling up to a superior point of height.

"Is that murder which the hawk is trying to do?" asked the medicine man.

"Why," said the boy, "he's acting according to his kind."

"So was I when I killed the white man in the camp," said Summer Day. "I was acting according to my kind. I inquired of the spirits, but they did not tell me that the thing was wrong. They would not speak. And, therefore, I did what all my kind would do."

"You lie," said the other sternly. "There are generous Indians as well as white men."

"A generous Indian is a generous fool," said the other. "A scalp is a scalp, to a red man, whether it be the scalp of a woman, a child, or a man. And a coup is a coup, even if it be counted on a toothless old man who is in his second childhood."

"Do you think," asked the white man curiously, "that you can talk me out of killing you?"

"I do not have to talk," said the other. "Either the spirits will help me, or else they will not. But I think that your hand is already helpless to slay me."

"You will see," said Messenger, and raised the gun.

The medicine man crossed his arms upon his breast and did not reply. Straight he looked into the muzzle of the ready gun, and Messenger vainly gritted his teeth together. He could not shoot the defenseless man.

He lowered the gun again and began to curse, softly, behind his teeth. Summer Day merely smiled.

"You have a knife and a gun," said he, "but after a moment, you will throw them both away, and you will fight me evenly, with your bare hands."

"Do you think so?" echoed the boy. "Almost one and a half of me could be made out of your bulk, Summer Day. You are almost as big as the horses you ride!"

"However," said the Indian calmly, "there is something that makes you even bigger."

"What is that?" asked the boy, half smiling. "What is it that the spirits have told you about me?"

"That you are proud," replied the medicine man. "And pride is like wind in a bladder. It blows up a man till he thinks that he is as tall as a tree. That is what you think, my friend."

At this, Messenger laughed aloud. He could not stop it. The combined frankness and insolence of the Blackfoot tickled him profoundly.

"Very well," said he, "and you think that I'll actually throw aside my knife and my gun in order to fight you on even terms?"

"You will," said the medicine man.

"What would I gain, except a chance to fight a much bigger man?"

"You would gain the one thing that you really want, a chance to feel me dying between your hands."

78

Messenger drew in a great breath. "Suppose that I do this insane thing, Summer Day."

"Oh, you will do it, my friend. Your eyes are turning red at this moment."

Suddenly, Messenger hurled the revolver far from him. After the gun, he threw his big and heavy knife. Then he made a gesture with both of his empty hands.

"Are you ready, Summer Day?"

The latter, grinning from ear to ear, looked after the knife and the gun and his eyes glittered triumphantly out at Messenger through the dusky hedge of hair that dropped over his face.

"Are you ready, my young friend?" he asked.

"I am ready," said Messenger.

"And so am I!" said the other, and suddenly passing his hand inside the belt which pinched his hips, he drew out not a big hunting knife but one with a slender blade. It was certain to puncture brain or heart with the ease of a bullet, and to kill as surely.

Messenger, with an exclamation, sprang back. Horror and disbelief filled him.

"Is that your good faith and your truth, Summer Day?" he exclaimed.

The latter, maneuvering to the side, had place himself instantly between the white man and the weapons which the latter had just discarded. Now he grinned with hideous satisfaction.

"You still can run, white man," said he. "Fool! Young brainless fool! You still can run like a deer out of the forest and let the people in the green hills see you coming, while the great Summer Day follows you, laughing, scorning such a child!"

The face of the boy turned crimson.

"I shall never do that," he said. "It is true that I have been a fool. I deserve to die for it."

"Die you surely will!" said the medicine man. "Like a proud young horse, too proud to carry a master, but just proud enough to have its neck broken, and to be eaten at a feast. Tough meat, but the Indians have strong teeth!"

He leaped suddenly forward as he spoke the last word. He had been in the very midst of a triumphant gesture which he broke off to jump in savagely, his lips stretched tightly back across his teeth.

Messenger, leaping aside and back, appeared to stumble. In any case, he had moved, it seemed, too slowly to avoid the knife thrust. But that sudden down sway of his whole body caused the knife to shoot harmlessly across his shoulder.

Instantly, he straightened. His movement was as swift as that of the dropping and rebounding hawk in the sky above them.

With his right hand he caught the knife arm of the medicine man at the elbow. Then, partially turning, with his left hand he gripped the knife wrist of the big fellow.

These actions, described in slow words, were performed almost simultaneously. One would have said that Summer Day was standing like a statue to allow the other to do as he pleased. But, as a matter of fact, he was moving with the speed of a leaping tiger.

But his arm was caught in a grip that ground the flesh against the bone. The tendons of his right wrist rolled and ground against the wrist bone, sending shooting, fiery pains along his arm. His fingers grew numb, and from them, as they loosened, the knife fell to the ground.

Messenger completed his maneuver by jerking the arm down over his shoulder and bending forward and down. Impelled by the weight of his own forward rush, the Blackfoot was lifted swiftly up and heaved in a great, clumsily flopping somersault through the air.

He would have broken his neck if he had landed on his

head. But twisting in mid-air, like a great cat, he landed on hands and knees. As he looked up, bewildered at what had happened, he saw that the white man stood smiling before him, with the little icicle of a knife glittering in his hand.

# 16

In the greatness of his despair, the medicine man gripped both his hands full of the turf. He had lost the battle, he saw. But great as his own fame and reputation were, his love of life was still greater. He did what any sensible man would have done. He bounded to his feet, and turning, he bolted for liberty in the direction of his horse.

He had not taken half a dozen strides before he knew that he was lost, when it came to a matter of speed. He threw a glance over his shoulder, and saw the white lad coming like a flung stone behind him, gaining with a terrible ease.

As he looked back, he saw the other smile, and threw the borrowed knife away. And then a ghastly panic streamed like ice through the blood of the Blackfoot.

He could see that Messenger would be contented with nothing but throttling him slowly, bit by bit, moment by moment, allowing him enough breath to linger out the hour of his dying.

But the battle pride of Summer Day was not yet exhausted. He had fought arm to arm and hand to hand against some of the greatest warriors of his day. In his boyhood, he had learned the complicated tricks of Indian wrestling until they were in his mind by rote, and still he had not forgotten. He told himself that even if the white lad had known one amazing trick, he was too young to have mastered the mysteries of the whole craft! And besides, Summer Day would not run from the empty hands of any man in the world.

Suddenly he flung himself to the ground.

He skidded through the grass. His speed made it seem greased. But, digging in his heels, and turning on his face, he checked the slide instantly and started to lurch up to his feet.

It was a very skillful stopping trick. He actually succeeded in getting to his feet without being taken at a disadvantage by the younger man.

And then, throwing back the hair from his face by a jerking motion of his head, he saw that the boy stood three strides away, at ease, smiling.

His hands were resting lightly on his hips. His head was high, and the first thing that the wary eye of the Indian noted was that these efforts had not made the breast of the youth begin to heave. For his own part, he was panting heavily.

"That was a bad fall, Summer Day," said Messenger. "Take a moment, now, to get your breath. Set your wits in order. You'll need them all."

Summer Day, glaring at him, could well believe what he had heard. All the cords of his right wrist were still burning, and shooting pains were still passing up his arm. Never had he felt such a grip as this which had been put upon him.

But there was something in the religion of his fathers. There was something, too, in sheer weight and bulk in a hand-to-hand encounter. Besides, he was himself as cunning as a fox.

So he struck his broad, painted breast with both hands, and his deep chest sounded like a drum.

"To you, spirits, my friends!" cried Summer Day, and went in to crush his foe.

He leaped forward, halted, and then with a half step onward, he struck with all his might and a closed fist at the head of the other. The white man barely drew back. It was an inclination of the body rather than an actual step; and yet the fist of the Blackfoot missed, whizzing by a fraction of an inch away. Again, and yet again, the medicine man struck, following in, getting his weight well behind the punches. And still he merely labored against the thin air.

He was instantly aware that he was no match for the slender boy at this game of fisticuffs. He strove to dive straight in for a wrestling hold, and as he did so, the poised right hand of the other dipped over and down, and a hammer stroke went home behind Summer Day's ear, and pitched him down on hands and knees.

There, as his brain cleared, the Indian lurched to his feet, looking wildly about him.

Messenger stood a little way off, and the cold, deadly smile was still on his lips.

"Wait a little, Summer Day," said he. "Let your head clear, and get your breath again. You'll need it all before the end."

And, as he finished, he flexed his lean fingers, as though already they were tingling for the throat of the Indian.

Summer Day shook his head like a bull.

"There was something in your hand. No hand is so like iron," said he. "But now you have exhausted all your tricks. Now you are mine. The spirits gave me the glory. I hear them speaking over my head. Your scalp is already drying in the smoke of my tepee fire!"

He made his stature greater as he talked. He went forward with short steps, one hand raised. More than once, before this, he had overawed his red-skinned enemies by these direct appeals to the spirits.

But Messenger continued to smile. Then he walked straight up to Summer Day and held out one hand.

"Here!" said he. "You may have the first grip. You are like a child or a woman. You are only a soft mass, without any tendons strung in your puppy fat. Now do what you can, Summer Day!"

No appeal to spirits could have the force of this calm contempt, this overbearing self-confidence. Summer Day looked up at the bright green of the trees, and it seemed to him that the blue of the sky above them was swirling before his eyes. He stared at the extended hand, suspecting some new trick.

But what trick could there be?

He stepped in close. Still the white man did not flinch. His breast struck the breast of Messenger. He was glaring down from his superior height into the eyes of the stranger, and those eyes, he thought, were as gray as iron.

A sudden shout of exultation burst sharp and short from the throat of Summer Day, like the bark of a dog, as he flung his arms around the comparatively frail body of Messenger.

The strain of his might, he felt, could crush in ribs of steel. He felt the meager back of the youth under the grip of his hands.

But though the body of Messenger gave, it would not break.

And suddenly all was not well with the chief.

The extended arm of the white man had passed under the pit of Summer Day's left shoulder. Now that arm whipped up and over the shoulder, and the hand of the white lad gripped the Indian beneath and around the jaw.

Like a bulldog's was that jaw of the medicine man. Once more the gripping hand of Messenger seemed to the chief like five constricting bands of iron—cold iron that shrinks and shrinks inexorably, crunching the flesh against the bone. He felt his cheeks ground in against his teeth.

With all his might, then, he strove to drag away the hand which held him by the jaw and was threatening to break his neck.

He gnashed his teeth in his fury. His breath began to come with a wheeze, like the wind in a broken bellows. But nothing could avail him to force that grasp to relax.

Then, like a desperate creature, he hurled himself to the ground in order that his weight might crush the body of the smaller man. But, at the moment of impact, a snaky twist of Messenger twitched him away from the danger, and it was the Indian who fell undermost, half stunning himself.

For one instant he lay still, without struggling.

He was striving to think, and his brain was failing him.

Far away above him, he could see the same hawk that he had noted earlier now sweep into sight over the head of the very same bird which had been fleeing from it before. The pressure of the chase, no doubt, had made the fugitive circle. Now it was heading for the trees and their sheltering tangle of branches with a desperate speed. Still faster came the hawk above it.

It turned over in the upper air. It gave several strong strokes of its wings, and then down it came bulletlike. The quarry dodged, almost as alert on the wing as ever. But this time it was outguessed. The hawk struck. The feathers flew in a little cloud, almost like a puff of smoke, and then away sailed the tyrant of the air, with a limp form trailing down from its talons.

Was not he, Summer Day, in like manner to become a weak, helpless thing in these murdering hands of iron?

# 17

That, in the first half second, was what he saw. And in the next, he was aware that by sheer physical might he could do nothing. The more he struggled, the farther back his head was thrust.

A little more, and he knew what would happen. The right hand of the white man would shift down, in a lightning slip, to the soft, exposed throat of Summer Day, and that would be the beginning of a quick end. For then, as surely as a wolf's grip ever cut off life at the throat of a quarry, just so would the hand of Messenger cut off the life which flowed in the bull throat of the medicine man.

In the second half-second, that was what Summer Day fully realized.

If, then, no force of hand could beat off this frightful wild catamount of a creature that clung to him, what could he do? His mind wildly passed over the ground on which they were struggling. And he remembered that, to the right, the ground sloped off very sharply toward the brink of the bank that hung above the river, far beneath.

There was a roaring in his ears.

Was it the sound of the blood struggling through his own arteries, or was it the voice of the river itself, calling to him?

And a desperate resolution came into the mind of the medicine man.

He looked up, in agony, to the wide blue arch of the sky.

"Sky People," he prayed in his mind, "give me strength to kill myself and take this white fiend with me to the same death!"

And he heard the voice of Messenger, hardly broken by panting, cool, cold, collected.

"Like a great soft hulk, without any force. Are you ashamed, Summer Day? You will die and rot in shame. There will be no dead horse to carry your spirit away on the hunting grounds of the Sky People. You are dying, Summer Day! Now, remember the white man in the camp, and how his eyes watched you. Remember how he screamed, Summer Day. Are you screaming now yourself? Scream again, Summer Day! Remember the white man, and the slow death!"

For, as he listened to the calm, sure, cruel voice, the utter horror of his position, the maddening helplessness of his mighty body, made a mighty wild cry rise up through the teeth of the medicine man.

That same horror gave him a new and sudden strength. It enabled him, floundering, to rise to his knees, and then to his feet.

Still, the white tiger clung to him, and the grinding power of the hand beneath his chin forced his head back until he was looking up at the zenith of the pale-blue sky.

The end was almost there. Aye, that moment it began, for the terrible grip of Messenger shifted that instant downward and closed into the cords and the straining muscles of the chief's throat.

Blackness swirled before the eyes of the medicine man. He no longer could breathe, yet it seemed to him that he was breathing, and that what he drew down deep were living flames!

All sense of direction was gone from him, so that he could not tell in which direction he was walking.

He made two or three steps. It seemed to him that the

slope went up before him. He turned about and struggled back in the opposite direction, and as he walked, he heard the exultant laughter of the man who was taking his life.

Then suddenly, the ground pitched down before him, and with all his might he hurled himself forward.

The white man, snakelike as before, twitched his body aside from the fall, but the force of the toppling bodies and the angle of the slope made them roll over and over again.

They gained momentum. They were spinning forward and down like a ball.

And suddenly the frightful grips of the other relaxed, and Summer Day found himself whirling like a wheel down toward the giant voice of the river.

All things, as he dragged down the first life-giving breath, seemed to be mixed, like madness, before his eyes. Then his battered wits came back, and he found that he was tumbling toward the verge of the river bank.

It was the thing which he had planned, but he had expected to take the white destroyer with him. Both of them would go whirling over the edge, and be dashed to death on the rocks.

That hope was lost to him.

Still, as he turned, he cast out his arms widely upon either side and one hand gripped a bush.

The power of his hand was such that the grip held, and the bush held him. It was half uprooted by the first wrench of the halt. It left the body of the medicine man dangling over the edge of the precipice, with the white face of the water dazzling beneath him.

And when he strove to pull himself up, he could hear a telltale ripping sound, and knew that the last of the roots were breaking.

And then, looking up, he saw Messenger running down toward him aslant on the slope, and with a face that reminded the Indian of the face of a hunting wolf.

At the same moment, the final deepest root of the shrub gave way, snapping like pack thread. And Summer Day dropped down.

He had no hope, but he struggled for life with the instinct of a wild beast. White men can despair easily. The Indian will struggle even if he be in the middle of rapids, and death be surely before him.

So Summer Day looked wildly beneath him and was aware that it was not a sheer drop, but that the cliff shelved out a little just below him.

Then as he struck a patch of straggling brush that clung somehow to the face of the bank, he spread-eagled, and arms and legs served as friction makers to check the impetus of his fall. Rapidly his fall turned into a reasonable slow descent. He gripped a handful of little branches here. He grasped at a narrow trunk, there. Leaves, dirt, and broken branches and whole shrubs, uprooted, showered down upon him.

And next he plunged over his head into icy water.

Straightening, he found that there was no pull of the watery hands of the current against him. Instead, he was in almost quiet water that lay under the hollow shoulder of the bank.

There he stood, and taking a great breath, before he stirred a step, he looked up at the narrow road through the sky which the ragged tops of the canyon walls fenced in across the heavens. To it he lifted his hands.

If piety never had come to him before, it came to him now. With his great arms stiffly stretched above him, and with his head thrown back, he uttered the first truly sincere prayer of his life.

Then he looked about him for a means of completing his escape.

But he was calm. There seemed to be in the soul of the medicine man the divine assurance that he would not die on this day at the hands of the white man, or the white water.

Then he saw what was to him as good as a great broad boulevard—a six-inch ledge well above the top of the stream, a ledge chiseled there by the superior force of the higher water, in the spring of the year when the mountain snows are melting the most rapidly. He was upon it at once, and found, presently, that it broadened.

Still breathing hard, but every moment with a lighter step and with a more joyous heart, he went up this narrow path, and found that he was rounding the side of the hill on which he had fought the white man.

He must not break out into the open.

For one thing, he would rather have walked into the living fire than to show himself with empty hands, beaten and a fugitive before the white man.

On the other hand, he dreaded more than the fire itself, or all the ridicule of his sharp-tongued fellow tribesmen, to face Messenger once more.

His throat still ached, bruised by the last grip. The blood still oozed inside his mouth, and his wrist ached and was swelling as though a bear trap had been closed over it.

There was no other man in the world like this. The Evil One himself lived in Messenger, surely, and the Evil One was to be avoided. Later, the Sky People would tell Summer Day what to do, but just now, he must secure his life.

What better than to hide in the very woods where he had fought the white man?

The latter was no cunning woodsman to find him out. How clumsily he had hidden, before, in the top of a tree, leaving himself helpless, with a telltale blue jay dancing about in the air to betray his hiding place. No, there in the woods the medicine man might hide himself and, afterward, perhaps work some "fire miracle" on the height, to restore the faith of his tribesmen.

So, with vague hopes before him, Summer Day climbed the bank, found himself among the trees near the edge of the woods, and instantly began to slink up the slope.

His mind steadied more and more.

He felt that he had come to a turning of the ways in his life. It might very well be that this day would so shame him that he would be cast out from among the warriors of his tribe. He would be degraded and despised as a maker of magic, if he could not command enough miracles to protect his own life. And what of the coward who fled from the foe?

But, looking up toward the blue through the tops of the trees, he placed his blind trust with the greater powers, and went his way.

# 18

Walking or running, stealing softly from tree to tree, and from brush to brush, the medicine man kept his eye sharp and his ear keenly attuned to all that passed around him, for the very thought of the young white man was now to him colder and more depressing than the chillest water in a January river. Death was a frightful thing, but the panic in the very bones of the Blackfoot would have made him leap another precipice to keep away from the hands of Messenger.

This panic, rising in him, several times almost made him burst out from the rim of the trees and take refuge among the massed numbers of his tribesmen who were scattered there. But he did not follow the impulse.

He went on, instinctively trusting in the dimmer light.

Now, through the branches of the trees, he could see the spectators on the outer hills, waiting. Sometimes they stirred, riding their horses back and forth. Weapons glittered—lances, and rifles balanced across saddlebows. It seemed to him that these restless creatures, who were his blood kinsmen, were like phantasms blown into the pages of a dream.

But they were his people, his place of power, and the thought of losing that place tormented the medicine man. What scorn they would heap on a coward.

But still, he was not prepared to die. Not the sort of a death that he must meet at the hands of the white lad. He told himself that he wanted a fighting chance, and no more, against a human being. This man was a ghost, and not a normal creature.

Such were the thoughts of the Blackfoot as he slipped along through the forest, and then, suddenly, came upon the sight of the pinto of the trapper, famous Henry Lessing.

The boy had ridden that horse. And, at the sight of the pony, the dazzled eyes of Summer Day conjured up the form of the boy, again, seated in the saddle. His heart stopped. Then, his eyes clearing, he discovered that the white man was not there.

What had become of him? For that matter, had he had time to come to this place from the site of the combat?

Another explanation, the true explanation, a moment later jumped into the mind of the medicine man. Messenger, seeing him fall down the almost sheer face of the cliff, and looking to the roaring, white face of the water, would have taken it for granted that the stream had devoured his enemy. His first impulse, then, might very well be to go take possession of the horse and the arms of his foeman. And, when he had found and mounted the little wild Indian pony, he would slowly ride around the edge of the wood, enjoying the plaudits of his friends, and greeted by the amazed and gloomy silence of all the disappointed Blackfeet.

No sooner had this thought come to Summer Day than he grew jubilant, and with reason. For he saw before him a clear path toward the reclamation of his fame. War Lance, who detested him, he knew, would not be able to exult on this day over the downfall of his hated rival for the leadership of the tribe. No, not if the slippery wiles of Summer Day could help him to the great end which he saw!

He paused only to slick the water from his leggings with both his strong hands. Then he bounded into the saddle on the pinto. He unsheathed the long-barreled Winchester—a beautiful weapon, and worthy of the hands of a chief! He gathered up the reins, and then delayed only an instant to replume the feathers in his hair, for they had stuck safe and fast in spite of the turmoil of the fighting.

These preparations done, he whirled the pony about. He straightened himself in the saddle. He took in a great breath that threw out his chest. He gathered his spirits like an animal about to leap, and with a ringing war cry, the shout of exultation, he burst on the horse from the edge of the woods where the boy had left him and into the open light of the afternoon.

All before him, as he appeared, the long line of his people greeted his appearance with a stunned silence, and then with an up-going, jubilant yell.

They swept forward. But he dashed straight on, heedless of their greeting, and with the rifle held stiffly, straight above his head, he plunged through that line of would-be questioners, and raced on across the hills toward his own camp.

They streamed behind him, those anxious, delighted braves. They yelled. They disturbed the air with the chorus of their shrill yippings.

And so into the camp they came.

What was happening on the farther side of the hill where the battle had been fought, they could not tell. They only knew that their own shouts had drawn away toward them all of their tribesmen, and that these were streaming after them across the hills as fast as they could flog their mounts along.

Straight through the camp dashed the medicine man, until he came to his own tepee. There he dismounted.

The strong sun and the wind of the gallop had dried his clothes, almost entirely. The warmth of the fire within the tent and the heat of his own body would soon finish the job. So he threw the reins to his youngest wife—he had taken three squaws, being a man of great Indian wealth—and retired within the flap of the lodge.

They would leave him alone.

No one would intrude rashly upon the chief medicine man of the tribe. For a few moments, he would be left entirely to himself. In the meantime, he made a little "medicine."

He burned some sweet-grass and purified himself with the smoke. He picked up a handful of earth and blew the dust away from the few little pebbles it contained, and then threw these up into the air several times, letting them fall back upon the flat of his stiffly extended palm.

It was a very simple way of making medicine. But his oldest wife—a bull for strength and a calf for wisdom— watched him with the same frozen interest which she always showed when permitted to overlook one of the rites which he performed.

Most of the pebbles bounced off his hand. There remained, finally, only seven.

"Seven!" he said aloud, in a deep and sepulchral tone. "Seven!" he repeated, and enjoyed the shudder of awe that ran through the body of his wife.

She, poor soul, looked as though she would gladly have been in any other place.

"There are people at the entrance," said he. "If any of them are chiefs, or famous warriors, let them come in."

There were, in fact, four men worthy to fill this description. To those four she gestured, and they entered hastily.

Inside the tepee the four were gratified and fed fat with marvels. The instant they entered, they had smelled the scent of the sweetgrass, which prepared them at once for hearing strange things—obviously medicine had been made.

"We must move our camp," said the medicine man. "We must move at once. Go out and tell the women to begin rolling up the lodge skins. Load the horses! The spirits have called to me, and we must go at once. Seven days— seven days—seven days we must march into the west!"

"And the young white man?" asked one of the chiefs, hardly daring to put a direct question.

"The young white man?" said the medicine man, recovering from his brief trance and shrugging his shoulders.

He made a gesture as though throwing something away.

"The young white man! The young leaves of the forest, fallen and dead before their time. The young white man! What is he to me? What is he to Summer Day, or to you— who are real warriors? I was about to take his life, while he begged for my mercy. I was about to take his life, when the spirits—"

He seemed to forget his auditors, lost in his semidivine contemplation.

"And then?" asked his oldest wife softly.

"And as I was about to run the knife over his throat—for I held him by the hair of the head, and his throat was tight, like the throat of a young calf about to be slaughtered—just at that time, I heard the spirits calling to me strongly, and so loud that I thought even the poor white boy must be hearing the cry! They called. They laid their thin, cold hands like winter wind upon my arms. They told me to spare the life of the white boy. They said that I must return at once to the lodge and there make medicine, and ask them what I must do.

"What was the scalp of a white child compared with the command of the spirits? Instantly, I threw him from me. He fell down in a heap on the ground and made weeping noises of joy."

# 19

In the meanwhile, young Messenger had planned to do exactly as the Blackfoot surmised, but he had not hurried to put his plan into execution. He had looked over the edge of the cliff and seen the man, as he thought, fall to as sure a destruction as though he had been plunged from the height of a tower toward a pavement. He almost thought that, a moment later, he had seen the glimmering body of the Indian hurled among the teeth of the rocks, instantly drawn under and disappearing forever.

And, for a time, he remained there on the lip of the ravine, meditating, and half sad. More than a runner for the great race, he had been trained for this battle. Now it was over, and the burden dropped from his mind.

He began to laugh suddenly, and the sound of that laughter, flowing strange and free, startled him, but not unpleasantly. All was beauty, and all was friendliness in this world. His thought ran back to the figure of the old trapper, and hung there, gently.

But there was goodness in all men, more or less. Only

the Blackfoot, Summer Day, was the exception. No, hardly even that. For as he remembered the grim desperation in which the big man had struggled for life, and then if not for life, to destroy himself with his conqueror, admiration for the red man came up in the heart of the boy, and a certain unexpected pity.

He was in no haste.

He even sat down for a time beneath the very tree in which he had lain along the branch, foolishly ambushing his enemy. The same blue jay fluttered above him, sailing back and forth across the clearing. Smiling up at the bird, he could understand now how it was that Summer Day had been able to detect him in his place of concealment. Nature, through the bird, had pointed a bright finger at him.

He put out his hand and passed the fingers through the short, thick grass, reveling in the touch. He lifted his head and sighed deeply with delight.

Then he saw the revolver which he himself had cast away.

It recalled him to the moment, and he stood up. Yonder, too, and close by, the broken blade of the Indian's knife glittered faintly among the blades of grass. He picked up the heavy silver of steel and cast it from his palm, hard-flung, into the trunk of the tree. There it stuck, quivering and humming wickedly.

He gathered up the revolver, then. He took up his own knife, which he had so foolishly discarded. He took up, as well, the little stabbing weapon with which the treacherous Blackfoot had delivered his second attack.

And, reflecting upon that, he remembered what the trapper had said about vice and virtue in an Indian. It was natural, was it not, that a red man should take as many advantages, through strength or through deceit, as a wildcat or a hawk in the air?

It was impossible for him to feel scorn at this moment.

And, finally, after he had done so many things, he was surprised to hear a loud shouting, and then a frantic yelling from the people who waited lower down on the mountainside, eager to get the first news of the battle.

What could have set them shouting so fiercely? Or was it with joy that they yelled. He was in no haste to find out.

It was some time after this that, making up his mind to start back, he decided that he would first of all pick up the pony which the unlucky Summer Day had ridden. Then, mounted upon this, he would round the side of the hill and get the trapper's pony. This he decided upon, and walked leisurely down the slope until he came to the outer verge of the trees, pressing through thickets and out into the startling light of the open day.

There he stood for a moment, warming himself, relishing the very strength of the rays that soaked like hot water through his clothes.

But he was surprised. He had thought that the whole wood was surrounded by observers. But now he could see not a single form upon the hills—only a few horsemen, in the distance, were making off toward the gate of the fort.

He was surprised, but he was not worried. The old trapper surely would be somewhere near, no matter what had drawn off the rest. Yes, surely Henry Lessing would not be far to seek.

He was right. As he started to saunter along the edge of the trees, he met Lessing coming in the opposite direction, riding a borrowed mustang, and leading the Indian's shaggy pony behind him.

At the sight of the boy, he uttered an exclamation, and reined in his horse.

It was an odd greeting, for he stared at young Messenger with a sort of horror that was almost like fear.

"What's the matter?" asked the boy. "You see that I'm out of it, safely enough?"

"Aye," said the trapper bluntly. "I see that you are out of it, right enough."

There was no pleasure in his tone.

"A bluff old fellow," said the boy to himself. "He won't show how glad he is that I'm the winner, but he's tickled pink, inside!"

He sprang onto the back of the Indian pony that was led behind.

"I'm going around this side to pick up your horse, Lessing," said the boy.

Lessing started, and looked hastily around. There was both amazement and scorn in his face.

"What horse?" he asked shortly.

"Why, the pinto that you lent me, of course," said the youngster.

"The pinto that I lent you?" repeated Lessing. "You didn't know that Summer Day rode that one off to his camp?"

"Rode it off! Summer Day will never ride a horse again!" said young Messenger.

"He won't? Was it his ghost, then? Or whacha think happened to the Blackfoot?"

Eagerness and more kindliness appeared in the eye of Lessing.

"He's down yonder in the teeth of those rocks," said Messenger, pointing toward the direction in which the angry dispute of the river roared after them.

"Boy, boy!" exclaimed Lessing, with an angry impatience. "Didn't I see him, with my own eyes, riding off yonder on my hoss? Didn't I hear with my own ears what the Injuns say is his story of the fight?"

Messenger drew the shaggy pony to a halt.

"What's his story of the fight?" he asked.

"That he got you down. That you begged for your life. That he promised to let you wear your scalp, and even that he wouldn't shame you, out of pitying such a young kid that had dared to fight him. And that he said he would let it go that you and him had changed weapons and horses, like friends, and that then he turned you loose. And—"

He halted.

For Messenger was laughing freely, easily, cheerfully in the sun; his very eyes were closed with mirth!

# 20

"He got away, after all?" said the boy.

"Summer Day managed to get down that bank and through the water? Well, if you saw him, of course, it's possible, and he managed to do it. But it's pretty hard to believe, all the same."

"I suppose maybe it is," said Lessing, dark of face.

"Summer Day is still alive, and the job to do all over again!" exclaimed Messenger. "Well, there's no hurry. I've had a taste of that business, and it'll never be hard to finish, of course. But wherever he went, I'll wager that he went fast!"

This made Lessing stare with a wider eye than ever. He remembered the flash of the warrior like a thunderbolt flying across the hills.

"Aye," said he. "He went fast enough. He went as fast as that hoss could carry him."

The boy nodded.

"He won't stop," said he. "He'll keep right on going.

He'll keep right on traveling for a considerable time, I suppose."

This time, the trapper actually gaped.

"As a matter of fact," said he, "they've struck camp and moved on—that whole section of the tribe. The same spirits that told the old liar not to cut your throat, they told him to move the tribe along."

"Ah, did they? And they'll keep moving, too, for a time, if he has his way," said the boy, and he chuckled.

The kindness left his face, and a sort of careless cruelty came there, instead. And, in his voice, there was a purr like the contented sound which a great cat makes by a fire.

"What it sounds like to me," said the trapper, "is that you never was put down by the Injun, after all—that he never had a chance to cut your throat at all!"

"He missed his stroke, the sneaking cur," said the boy cheerfully. "He's not a fighting man, Lessing. He's a bungler. You could count ten, almost, every time he made a move. He let me know beforehand what he was going to do. He signaled with his eyes, or with his shoulders, or with his hands. You could read his mind half a second ahead."

He laughed again at the memory, and the rich sound of that mirth made the trapper blink. This was not the voice of the lad that had gone up there into the woods to fight for his life.

"Son," said he, "suppose you tell me every blessed thing that happened between you and that Injun?"

And the boy told him, not in haste, but slowly. He dwelt upon the incidents, often laughing, until he came to the point in which he described the throttling of the big red man.

The trapper, during that recital, stroked his throat once or twice. But then he shook his head.

"Tell me," said the boy curiously. "Don't you belive what I've said?"

"Son," said Lessing, "I believe every word that you've told me. It's hard to believe, I grant you. But I believe. Like gospel. And now I'm gunna give you some good advice."

"I'm ready to hear anything you have to say, Lessing."

"Then listen to this: Never tell this yarn to another man in the world!"

"They wouldn't believe, you mean?"

"They'd never believe."

"Well, I'll have to jog along after that tribe, I suppose. I'm no trailer, but I suppose that they'll not be hard to follow, if there are enough of them."

"You can't do that. Meeting them down here by the fort is one thing. If Summer Day has anything that he fears about you—and by your yarn he has aplenty—the minute you heave in sight, he'll pass a word to the young bucks, and they'll come out in a swarm and sting you to death!"

Messenger squinted his eyes, considered. Nothing disturbed him, now. He was at ease. Nothing could excite him.

"That sounds like a good prophecy," said he. "I'll have to take my time about finishing him off. And it won't be hard."

And he laughed again, with that little purr in the voice which had troubled the trapper before this.

"What are you going to do, son?" said he.

"They'll think that I'm a coward, if I go back to the fort?" said the boy.

"They'll think just that, and they'll think it hard. Don't go to that fort!"

"Where should I go, then?" Messenger was amazed.

"Any place but there."

"Because I'm to be afraid of the half-breeds—and the whites there—or is it the Indians, Lessing?"

"All of 'em, and something more. You think that you're like other folks, now."

"Ah, but I am, Lessing."

"You're not. You're a whole wide mile from bein' like other men, and there ain't nothin' but fire gunna be knocked out of rock when you meet up with them."

"What sort of fire, man?"

"Why, cutthroats, and bullets through the brain, and that sort of thing."

"Ah, I'd never hurt anybody, man. There's no harm in me—if they leave me alone!"

Suddenly, Lessing was shouting, the veins swelling in his forehead.

"Don't you see it?" he cried. "They'll think that you're just an ordinary dog, now, and that they're the wild wolves! Nothin' in the world could ever keep them from tryin' to put teeth into you. Nothin' in the world!"

"Ah, well," reflected the boy, "that'll soon be over. But I'll never strike back too hard, Lessing. I'll promise you that!"

# 21

Having gone out to battle almost an assured hero, Messenger came back a presumptive coward. After his dealings with the two Indians in the fort, there was not a man within the palisade who would have matched himself against this young man of mystery. When he returned from the battle on the hill, there was hardly one who did not feel that, in some way, Messenger was beneath his contempt. He had been apparently guilty of the greatest sin, the one unforgivable failing. Nature had undoubtedly endowed him with great gifts which had been perfected by scientific training. All the more shame, then, that he had failed in a crisis and begged his life from an Indian brave!

For the story of the medicine man was everywhere believed.

Red men have their faults, but in one thing they are almost religiously believed—and that is when they recount the tale of their battles. Too much depends upon this truth. When the coup stick is passed around at the feast and the warriors are invited to enumerate their deeds, the man who tells a single real falsehood has damaged every other man in the tribe. If he claims six coups instead of five, which actually belong to him, all the true holders of six coups are injured by his rivalry, and the honest possessors of five are falsely eclipsed. Therefore, all ears attend to the warrior who talks. A falsehood, once detected, makes the liar worse than a woman in the tribe from that time henceforward. His wives scorn to stay in the tepee of such a creature. His friends desert him. He is included in no war party.

For these reasons, an Indian's battle-word could be trusted scrupulously and there was only one man in the fort who doubted the story of the medicine man, and that was Henry Lessing. Even he would hardly believe what the boy had told him. An instinct, merely, assured him that it would be harder for Messenger to lie than for an Indian.

But Messenger, coming back to the fort, found all eyes cold and hostile, and walked, surrounded by sneers.

He paid no heed to them. It made little difference that he had failed to kill the red man. At least, he had demonstrated his measureless superiority, and the finishing of the work which must be done was not worth consideration. So, at all events, he felt.

He went up to the store with his friend, Lessing. The whisky stall was always open. The rest of the store was only unlocked in the mornings, when the trafficking was done. But as for whisky, that was another matter. Rare profits flowed into the coffers of the trader from the sale of the liquor at all times of day and the night. Only, when the sun set, the Indians were forced to leave the fort, the gate was locked, and only the whites and a few half-breeds remained. Money bought the liquid poison then, or fine furs, usually taken off the person. Desparr was scrupulously honest during the day, never cheating more than his good wits allowed him to do. But outside of office hours, as it were, at the whisky counter he took in what he could. He traded whisky for anything from beaded moccasins to good new rifles. And his profits here ranged anywhere from a hundred to a thousand per cent above his daylight trafficking.

Beside the counter, over which the whisky was ladled into small cups, there was a little room usually lighted with two lanterns which were fed with the oil of fat. The light they cast was dim; the smell of the burning fat was far from pleasant, and the air was always wreathed with the pale-blue drifts of smoke from long pipes. But there was enough illumination to show the spots on cards, and here the gambling went on. Sometimes a blanket was unfolded on top of a table or, better still, on the floor, and dice were rolled. But usually cards were the game. Men came in here with three years' value in furs and went out after a single morning with their pockets empty. It hardly mattered. Life lasted forever—unless a bullet stopped it—and hands which had been filled out of the treasures of the wilderness would very soon be replenished.

There was never a bigger crowd for whisky than on the evening after the fight, for three boats and seven white men, all in a party, had come up to the fort. The supplies which they brought fairly gorged the magazine of the place. And the heart of Louis Desparr waxed big and warm with hope.

Money was current, now. It was fairly in the air. And Louis told his wife, who served the liquor across the counter, to make the drinks of whisky big—the cups should fairly brim with the stuff. Often what the traders had earned during a three or four months' journey returned to him, via the whisky route, before the next morning.

When young Messenger saw the swirl of people going into the saloon, for that was what it really was, though not in name, he insisted that the trapper should go in with him. He wanted to buy a drink, and at the same time, he wanted to pay Lessing for his horse which the Indian had stolen.

"I'll take that hoss he left with you, son," said the other.

"He's a ragged rat, you wouldn't want him," insisted Messenger.

The trapper merely laughed.

"D'you know who the medicine man is?" he asked.

"I suppose I do."

"If a slick-lookin' hoss would've served him better, he would've had a slick one. But he knows what he's after. That rough rat will probably carry twice as much weight twice as far and twice as fast as my pinto. I won't lose by the trade, if you want to make it."

"But there's a rifle, and other things in the saddlebags."

"Nothin' worth talkin' about. No, sir, if I get Summer Day's pet war hoss, I'll be satisfied, all right."

"Then come in and have a drink, anyway."

"Look here, son. How much of this trade whisky have you drunk?"

"I've never drunk a drop of anything, in all my days."

"Never a taste?"

"Never a taste. I've been training for today all my life, and now that today's over, I'm going to celebrate the way other people do."

The trapper merely chuckled.

"You come and have that taste, then," said he. "I reckon that you won't want more'n one!"

So young Messenger went into the whisky shop with his friend.

They stood at the counter at the side of the game room, and the intent faces of the gamesters and the tang of the tobacco smoke seemed all foolish signs to the boy. However, he was intent upon learning. There were ways in which the rest of the world enjoyed itself, and he was going to try them out.

The drinkers faced one another.

"Here's to you, son," said the trapper, grinning over the edge of the cup.

"I say the same," said the boy, smiling in the new way which had come to him. "Here's to you, Lessing. You've been a friend to me. And I've never had a friend before."

"Hold on," said Lessing, lowering the cup. "Not even a playmate?"

"Playmate? I've never played a game in my life," said the other, shrugging his shoulders. "Except boxing. And it wasn't a game, the way I had to box!"

Lessing stared.

"Then—here she goes down!" said he.

And they drank.

Lessing, slowly replacing his cup on the counter, began to grin. For the boy had gripped the edge of the big board and hung there, making odd faces.

First, fire had run down his throat and still was burning fiercely in the pit of his body. Then nausea struck his stomach and his brain with a double blow, as he got the full, awful taste of the stuff. But, after that, as his mind spun into a thin, colorful mist, a hot feeling of careless joy followed.

He was amazed.

He looked up from the counter and began to laugh.

"Take another one. I want to buy it," said the boy.

"I'll take no more. You come outside with me and get some fresh air into you," advised the trapper.

"Go outside? I'm only beginning inside!" answered the youngster.

"You might as well jump off a cliff as to drink any more of that stuff," stated Lessing. "Why, the hardest of them go down after a few shots of it! It ain't whisky. It's poison. It takes getting used to. Honest whisky ain't like this stuff. You come along with me, before you get sick!"

"I'll stay here," said the boy, with a sudden and gloomy stubbornness. "I'm going to stay here and have another one."

"Don't do it," pleaded Lessing.

"I'm going to," insisted young Messenger. "Will you stay with me?"

Lessing hesitated. He knew what whisky, such as was served at that post, will do to unaccustomed brain, but he decided that there might be a better way of meeting the problem, and that would be to persuade his friend Desparr to close up the counter for that evening, before trouble started.

So he went off to find the trader, and young Messenger went back inside the shop.

He found a chair in a corner and sat down.

The taste in his mouth was horribly unpleasant, but a giddy sense of happiness had mounted to his brain.

# 22

The young man had another drink, and the mighty slug of hard liquor and adulterants smote his brain like a hammer on an anvil. His head swayed a little; and things began to waver before his eyes.

"I'm weak," said he to himself. "I'm strong in other things, but in this, I'm weak. Practice is the only thing that will teach me."

And he took another.

He was barely back in his chair, after this potation, when another delegation of three came into the room. Two of them found stools. The third was left without one.

He was one of those big fellows all of whose muscles seem hardly enough to manipulate their great frame of bone. His name was Buck Chandler. He was hardly twenty-five, and he had traded, trapped, hunted buffalo, hunted men on the trail, and committed enough crimes to send half a dozen men to the hangman's rope. Yet, out there on the rim of civilization, people were often glad to have Buck Chandler about. He was as strong as a mule and as enduring. And if a battle came the way of the party which he had joined, they could count on him as upon four ordinary fighters. It was Buck Chandler who now found himself without a place to sit down, and he looked around the room with his bright little animal eye ready to make trouble.

Resting his elbows on the edge of the counter, he faced the little crowd. And, almost with the first glance, he spotted the tenderfoot, in the gray woolen clothes and with the pale face which could not have been long upon the frontier. A muttered question over his shoulder brought from Mrs. Louis Desparr a rapid account of the recent battle between the white boy and the Indian medicine man—the account which the great Summer Day had himself spread.

Buck Chandler grunted and strode straight across the room to the place where the boy was sitting, smiling vacantly into the smoky air.

"How come you sit when there's a man standing?" asked Chandler.

The boy started to answer, but the words came to his lips in a mere faltering stammer.

"Get up and get quick!" said Chandler, and he reached his hand for the collar of young Messenger.

The latter laughed, and gripped at the extended arm. He should have been able to seize it, just as it was in motion, at the wrist, and at the elbow. And, a moment later, Mr. Chandler would have been upon his back on the floor—or nursing a broken arm!

But the hands of Messenger refused to obey his will. He saw what he wanted to do. He knew exactly how to do it, but a singular lethargy possessed his muscles and he made merely a feeble, pawing gesture.

Buck Chandler, the next instant, had him by the collar of his coat and flung him flat on the floor. Messenger lay sprawling for a moment, then picked himself slowly up to his hands and knees. When he turned, he found that Chandler was waiting, his feet spread, a brutal grin of pleasure upon his lips.

Messenger struck straight out. That good left hand of his, carefully educated for so many years, should have found its mark on the edge of Chandler's jaw. But it was no longer a good hand. It was feeble, slow, and useless. Buck Chandler brushed it aside with contempt and smote Messenger fairly between the eyes.

The force of the stroke knocked Messenger's head back and he flopped heavily, inertly, upon the packed dirt floor of the shack.

"You've knocked him silly, Buck," said someone.

And a hard-faced trapper broke in: "We'd oughta bring him around. Maybe a coupla throws in a blanket would help him a pile to come to."

They jumped at the idea. Someone produced a buffalo robe, and Messenger, just beginning to stir feebly, was dragged outside and thrown into the robe. Half a dozen strong pairs of hands grasped the edges of the blankets, and as the men leaned back, and the robe came suddenly taut, with a popping sound, Messenger was flung high into the air. His loose body revolved there, head over heels, and he descended again on his head with a force that well-nigh broke his neck.

The blanket yielded under the impact, was instantly jerked tight again, and up went Messenger, higher still, spinning still more rapidly. He began to recover his wits, but half stunned as he was, amazed, not knowing what was happening, a wild yell of fear, of distress, broke suddenly from his lips.

It was answered by a demoniac chorus from below. To torment a victim was a delight; but to wring from the unlucky man such a cry was more than could be hoped. Tugging and jerking at the blanket in unison, they kept Messenger most of the time helplessly in the air.

People gathered to watch, laughing and shouting, until old Henry Lessing came up. He laughed in his turn, until he made out who the victim was.

At once he interfered, and at the sharp sound of his

111

commanding voice two of the torturers suddenly dropped the edge they were holding and stepped back.

Messenger, landing headfirst in the robe again, slid down the sharp slant and rolled head over heels upon the hard ground.

There he lay still, utterly unconscious, while Buck Chandler approached Lessing with a snarl.

"Who are you?" he said. "Who made you the judge and the jury to tell us what we're gunna do to a sneakin', lyin', cowardly tenderfoot that we don't want around Fort Lippewan?"

Lessing was not perturbed by the reputation of the bully. He looked steadily back into the eyes of the young giant and answered: "I'm Hank Lessing. I oughta have twenty-five, thirty, years more experience and sense than you have, Chandler, and I reckon that I have."

Chandler laughed loudly.

"You're an old loon," said he, "and I'm here to tell you about it."

"Words," said Lessing, "don't hurt me. No words that you can say will make a fool of me, young man!"

It looked, for a moment, as though Chandler would strike the trapper, but he changed his mind at the last moment. The difference in their size was too pronounced; and besides, those dry, hardy, old frontiersmen like Lessing were sometimes amazingly agile and fast with their pistol hands.

So Chandler went back into the saloon, still snarling over his shoulder, but attempting no further violence.

And the thing he had done to young Messenger was not criticized. There had been twenty pair of hands aching to put Messenger in his place; but memories of what he had done that morning to the two young Indian braves had held them back. Now he had been bludgeoned to the ground, and the onlookers were glad of it. By tomorrow, they would make the fort so hot for him that he would be sure to start back for civilization.

That was the universal feeling.

Only Henry Lessing remained out there in the dewy coolness of the evening and watched over the boy until Messenger opened his eyes and, groaning faintly, sat up. He raised a hand to his forehead. It was blurred and sticky with the red that had run down from the cracked skin.

Lessing, in the meantime, helped him to his feet and took him straight off to his own room in the fort. It was just beside the ones used by Desparr and his squaw, and Desparr himself came in for a moment to look at the boy.

"He's got only what's comin' to him," said Desparr. "A sneakin' young coward, and you're a fool to waste your time over him, I tell you, Hank!"

Lessing looked sharply up over his shoulder—for at the moment he was kneeling beside the form he had stretched on the bunk.

"Louis," said he, "if I was you, I'd sashay right out of this room before the things that you say might be understood by somebody."

"You think maybe that he'd throw a scare into me. Henry?" asked the trader.

"Louis," replied the trapper, "the fact is that he licked the hide off of that lyin' red Injun. You won't believe that he did, but I've told you the fact. Now, get out of here before he comes around and spots you in his mind. And he's got a memory. Some of the boys here in the fort, they're gunna find out what he can do!"

Louis Desparr, looking down at the still bleeding face of the boy, grinned broadly.

"He got enough," he said. "I heard him holler, clear up here. He had the wits pretty near scared out of him. A drunk, too. Yeah, you've picked up a fine, big, clean-hearted boy, all right."

113

But Lessing paid no heed to him, beyond giving him a warning glance.

There was nothing in that glance that would have stirred Desparr, however. But Messenger, suddenly groaning again in his torpor, made a flashing movement of his hand. Instantly, a knife glittered in it. The fingers of the hand relaxed at once and the knife fell with a clatter to the floor; but the speed of the movement, the deadly nature of the weapon, and the fact that it had been drawn when the man was only half conscious, made Desparr gape.

He turned upon his heel and left the room at once.

# 23

It was a night which Lessing was never to forget.

Another half hour passed before he discovered that the eyes of the boy were open and that he was staring straight above him at the ceiling of the room.

"How does it come, my lad?" asked the trapper.

Slowly, Messenger turned his head, and the look in his eyes made Lessing wince. In place of answering with words, the boy extended his hand, gave that of Lessing a long grip, and then returned to his staring at the ceiling.

The trapper did not speak for some time. But he could see the breathing of Messenger increase rapidly. The face of the lad turned crimson, and then white. The last fumes of the whisky were gone from his brain, but he was left in a mental torture that caused his hands to grip into fists.

"Lie easy," said Lessing, at last. "Lie easy, and don't you worry none."

A slight, impatient movement of the hand answered him.

"Try to sleep," said Lessing.

The boy nodded. "Yes," he said. "I have to sleep. I must be fit in the morning—" He raised himself upon one arm and looked about him. "This is the only bed you have, Lessing," he observed.

"I could make myself comfortable for a night on a chunk of rock," Lessing assured him, with truth enough.

But young Messenger stood up. "If you'll spare me one blanket—"

"Aye, half a dozen, if you want 'em. But stay there on that bunk and get your sleep."

"I've slept on hard floors as long as I can remember," answered Messenger, and coiling the blanket around him with a single flip of his hand he lay down near the wall.

In ten seconds, while Lessing was still protesting, he could tell by the regular rise and fall of the youngster's breast that he was either sleeping or expertly shamming sleep. But he guessed the former to be the case, and this amazed him a great deal more than anything he had yet seen the boy do, or heard of him performing. To have throttled that huge fellow, Summer Day, was really as nothing compared with this feat. One moment, Messenger had been lying on the bunk, writhing with a fiercely controlled shame and hate; the next, he had composed himself on the floor and was soundly asleep. With incredible power of will, he had composed his body, relaxed every nerve, and now he slept like a baby, with an unperturbed face!

He would not sleep long, Lessing could guess as he watched the inert figure. Anyone who could relax as perfectly as this was sure to get his completed repose in half the time that normal humans require. And Lessing, walking up and down the floor, and even stamping upon it, made sure that young Messenger was utterly unconscious.

When he was confident of this, he went into the adjoining room to speak with his host, and found Louis Desparr smoking his last pipe of the day, and sitting beside the fireplace. For the night had turned cold, and in the chinks of the wall was the whine of a rising wind.

Mrs. Louis Desparr, despising chairs, was squatted in a corner of the room on a folded robe and doing bead work on a deerskin shirt with incredibly rapid hands. Her fingers seemed far too big, but the little needle glanced and flashed like a machine.

When she saw the white man enter, she rose at once. She placed a chair for him and stood behind it, looking from Lessing's face to that of her lord, for instructions.

Lessing waved her away.

"I'm not sitting down," he said. And to Desparr: "Louis, there's gunna be an explosion around this here fort, and the time of it will be somewhere about the middle of the morning, when there's a crowd to see the damage done."

Desparr looked steadily at him, his eye glassy with weariness. His thought only half followed the words of his trapper friend, for he was now looking rather dreamily into the future.

This had been a great day in his life. The arrival of the new stock, the presence of well-known hunters and traders, and the fact that more than half the Blackfeet, including the famous War Lance, remained to trade in spite of the sudden departure of the medicine man of the tribe—all these things convinced Louis Desparr that the days of profit taking had arrived. He was looking at the future, and he paid little heed to the words of his friend.

"We get our crowds pretty early, after the store opens," he observed.

"Then the explosion may come early," said Lessing. And he pointed toward the next room.

"You still got that blasted kid on your mind?" demanded the trader.

"Oh, Louis," said the trapper, "you act like one that won't believe he's been blowed up till he falls down out of the air, again, and gets his fool neck broke. I've warned you three times. I ain't gunna waste no more words on you!"

At this, Desparr roused himself. "What d'you want me to do?" he asked. "Throw him out of the fort and lock the gates on him?"

"It wouldn't do any good," said the trapper. "He'll either climb over or he'll burrow under. Or else he'll pull up the poles and walk in through a gate of his own makin'."

Desparr snorted, and his contempt was real.

"Let him go and try it. But if you don't want us to throw him outside, what do you think we should do with this young hero of yours?"

Lessing shook his head.

"You're gunna groan, but if I was you, I'd throw young Buck Chandler out of Fort Lippewan, and I'd do it fast, and throw him far, and tell him that he wasn't never wanted back inside again!"

"Would you?" gasped Desparr. "What you talkin' about, Hank? That Chandler is one of the toughest hombres north of the Rio Grande. I never seen a harder man than that young feller is."

"Louis, you won't take my word, but compared with young Messenger, he's softer'n new-fallen snow. He's softer than the down off the breast of a baby duck. That's how soft he is compared with Messenger."

"You've gone loony," answered Desparr, totally unconvinced. "What'll he do?"

"He'll kill Chandler, I think," said the trapper, lifting his head and looking at the wall and through it toward the future. "He'll pretty sure kill Chandler."

"Chandler's got half a dozen murderin' bad young fellers around him," remarked the trader.

"If they step in, he may kill them, as well. And every gent that was in your whisky room, he's likely to remember them and polish them off, too."

At this, Louis Desparr leaned back in his chair and laughed long and loud.

"Why, if he does that, he oughta have a chance to get away with 'em. I won't interfere, none!"

Lessing drew in a great breath.

"I've warned you the last time," he said.

"Why, Hank, you don't talk with no sense, when you talk about that boy! What's he done? Floored a coupla fool braves that was already half drunk, likely. And then he's taken water from a Blackfoot, and then he's got himself licked by Chandler, fair and square stand-up fight. And after that, he's got himself throwed in a blanket. And then my partner, Lessing, he goes and takes this young skunk and lays him out in his own room. Henry, I sure respect your ideas usually, but not this idea at all!"

Lessing went back to the door.

"I'll do my best," said he. "I'll try to keep close to him and keep track of him. I'll lock the door and put the key in my pocket—but I figger that tomorrow is gunna give you and all of us a terrible shock!"

Desparr shrugged his shoulders. He settled in his chair to finish off his good-night smoke, and Henry Lessing went back to his own room.

He looked at the sleeper, who apparently had not stirred, and then locking the door and putting the key in his pocket, and making sure that the window was too small to allow a man to squeeze through it, he lay down to sleep.

# 24

When Lessing wakened in the morning, he instinctively reached into his pocket, and sighed with relief when he found that the key still was there. Then he looked toward the door, which was closed—toward the window, through which the sun was pouring brightly, and showed that he had far overslept himself.

Last of all, he looked toward the guest of his room, and found that he was not there.

This discovery, he would not believe for a time. He leaped at last to his feet and looked about the room wildly, as though he thought that he must find the boy stowed somewhere in a corner.

But there was no sign of Messenger. He was gone like a whiff of wind.

Running to the door, the bewildered trapper found that it was locked, just as he had left it.

He rushed next to the window, but dust lay thick upon the lower part of the embrasure, and it was certain that no man could have gone through without disturbing that dust.

Lessing rushed out to find Desparr; but Desparr was long since gone from his room. The store had been opened and the trading of the day was going full blast.

Down into the store passed Lessing, more excited than ever. And he hunted up his friend, Desparr, at once.

The store was filled. War Lance himself was there, stepping through the crowd like a giant wading through a turbulent river. He went slowly, and the throng divided its tangles before his coming.

To him, however, Lessing gave not a glance.

He leaned across the counter before the trader, actually elbowing two angry braves aside.

"Have you seen young Messenger?" he asked.

The other grinned. "Not hide or hair of him," he said.

"He faded out of my room, last night. Without a key, he unlocked the door and locked it again, and got away," panted Lessing.

"He must've took wings and flown, then," said Desparr; "and I reckon that he'll keep right on flying till he gets pretty far away from Fort Lippewan. He ain't wanted here, and he knows it, I guess."

Lessing went out into the inclosure.

Vainly he ran his glance over the faces of the swaying crowd. There was no glimpse of Messenger among them. A thought had come to him, that perhaps his apprehensions were entirely wrong, and that the boy really had not been in an agony of shame and rage when he lay on the bunk the preceding evening, but was overcome by fear. Fear, also, might have made him flee from the fort before he had to encounter the rude hands of big Chandler again. In that case, Desparr was right. And Lessing hoped he was.

He grew easier, after this.

And then, a moment later, he had a view of Chandler, head and shoulders above the crowd, making his way through the hurlyburly by weight and elbowing. In the wake of the ruffian, the trapper allowed himself to drift. If trouble came, almost undoubtedly it would come to Chandler. And he, Lessing, might, therefore, be in time to ward off violence. Though he rather doubted even his own influence upon Messenger.

To make the danger greater, Chandler was not alone. He

was the point of the wedge which cut through the crowd. Behind him went three of his associates, characters as depraved as himself. What would happen if their united weight fell upon young Messenger?

For half an hour, Henry Lessing wandered behind the quartet. Then, suddenly, it paused like a craft that has put its nose upon a rock. There was a rapid, excited muttering among the Indians, and these quickly gave back so that a small, open circle was left. By making this space, the crowd was compacted so thick upon the rim of the circle that Lessing could not break through it. He could only look helplessly on between heads and shoulders and see, facing Chandler, the form of Messenger himself!

For there he was, a little paler than ever, but erect, easy, and meeting the eye of Buck Chandler with a steady gaze.

"Here's the tenderfoot again!" shouted Chandler, and laughed. "Get out of my way, rat, before you're stepped on." And he struck out with the flat of his heavy hand.

He might better have struck at a dancing leaf in the wind. Only the air was cuffed aside, and the iron fist of Messenger went home with an audible thud.

It put down Chandler as though he had been sandbagged.

"He clubbed me!" said the dazed voice of Chandler. "Smash him, you fellows—"

He hardly needed to ask.

Straight past him charged his three adherents in a solid line. One of them was drawing a gun. The other two trusted to their fists, and as a yell of excitement went up from the bystanders, Lessing saw the two forces meet.

He squinted his eyes, horrified. He saw a revolver swung upward, grasped by the barrel, and the next instant he saw the tawny head of the boy, for which the blow was aimed.

But the man of the clubbed revolver went down, that

instant, like a stack of cards struck by the wind, though Lessing could not see the punch which had dropped him. A knife flashed, and its wielder the next instant was staggering backward, his face already blurred with crimson. The fourth of the number, seeing what had happened to his fellows, turned to run, but the solid human wall checked him, and he was struck down from behind.

Still, the battle was not ended. Buck Chandler was lurching to his feet again. He had tried his bare hands and found them wanting. Now he would try what was in the force of powder and ball. The revolver was in his hand as he rose.

This was seen by Lessing, but, the next moment, a shift in the shouting crowd threw several heads between him and his line of vision. Men were fighting and struggling to get back from the naked weapon. No bullet could miss. If it failed to strike the target aimed at, it was sure to drive on into the flesh of the human wall which stood around.

But still there was not an explosion of a gun.

Instead, Lessing saw a gun thrust upward high into the air. It was the hand of Buck Chandler which held it, and another hand, lean and narrow, was fastened upon it at the wrist.

That imprisoning hand was seen to work suddenly to the right and left—and the gun dropped from the unnerved fingers of Chandler.

Now Lessing could see the face of the bully. It was contorted with fear. His lips parted. He screamed terribly—the prolonged cry of a man in agony.

What was happening to him, Lessing could not make out. He could only see the dreadful, contorted face of the big man, and then, horribly clear in the sudden silence as the scream ended, there was a dull, crackling sound unlike anything he had heard.

It brought from Chandler another shriek; and then he disappeared, sinking to the ground.

No one spoke immediately.

Lessing half expected a great outcry from among the warriors, for Chandler was thoroughly hated by the Blackfeet for many reasons. But there was not a cheer. The warriors stood about with a stunned look. And presently, Lessing could see the boy clearly.

For the crowd was falling away to either side before him, as though all whom he faced half expected that they might become the next victims.

There was only one whisper from nearby, in the Blackfoot tongue: "The iron hand! There is big medicine in his hand!"

But the boy walked slowly forward through the opening lane and, seeing Lessing, made straight toward him.

He came to Lessing and laid a hand on his arm. It was a friendly gesture, but enough excitement remained in the boy to make that grip bite into the arm of Lessing, to the bone.

"We might go and have breakfast together," said the boy.

"Breakfast," said Lessing hoarsely. "Breakfast, with those fellows loose and plotting how they can murder you?"

"They?" said the boy, with a careless shrug. "I don't think that they'll ever lift their hands again—not even from behind!"

# 25

They went back, accordingly, away from the center of the crowd, and when they were apart, Henry Lessing said: "What's happened to them, Messenger?"

"Something that will make them feel unlucky for a long time," he said.

"What did you do to Chandler? I thought I heard a noise, like bones breaking?"

Messenger shrugged again.

"Look!" he said suddenly. "I thought that there were no ruffians in the world. All at once, I thought that the world was full of my friends. I sat there and swilled whisky like a beast. That's what it is to be like other men. To be a beast is to be most like them! I see that now. I didn't see it then. I've met one man I could call a friend. And he's a man who has spent a great deal of time by himself, who prefers the wildest mountains to life with other men! And you're right, Lessing. I see that now. You were right about the Indians, too. They are wild and they're savage. But they would not take advantage of a sick man. They might scalp him and kill him. But they would not disgrace and shame him, as Chandler and the rest of his pack did to me, last night. I want only one thing, and that's the names of the others who were with him!"

"You'll never get it from me," said Lessing.

He felt exceedingly uneasy, because of the question

which had been asked. Something, beyond a doubt, had happened in the nature of Messenger, since the day before. He had come to the fort with the hardness of an automaton, a machine-made creature. He had passed from that into a reckless springtide of abandoned joy in living and affection for all his fellow creatures. All in a moment, in a single night, he had passed beyond this and grown into what could only be called a soured maturity.

"I won't need to find out the names from you," said the boy, after a moment. "They'll tell me their names themselves."

"Nobody will tell you, Messenger."

"You're wrong," said the boy, with a click of his teeth. "If I let it be known, for instance, that I'll pay a hundred dollars a name—or even fifty—or perhaps even ten—do you think that some cur won't come forward to tell me everything that he knows?"

His lips curled as he spoke, and the face of Lessing grew hot. In this condemnation of all mankind he felt a peculiar interest. He could see the truth that was in it. In any crowd, there is very apt to be some craven who will sell himself.

"And if no one tells me," said the boy, "still, I think those fellows will be uneasy. They've seen what's happened to Chandler and his crew. And any trapper or trader who leaves the fort within the next day, without having finished his business, will be a man for me to trail!"

"What will you do when you catch them?" asked Lessing.

"Those four," answered Messenger. "I wanted to kill them, every one. The next that I come on—well, I don't know. It's a wild land, Lessing, and one has to adopt wild ways to suit it."

His lips quivered as he spoke. Anger had seized him at the mere thought.

"Some of those fellows threw you up in a blanket," said Lessing. "And now you want to run a knife into every one of them. Is that reasonable, son?"

"It may not be that," replied the boy. "I don't know what I'll do until I see them."

Lessing fell into a brown study.

When he looked up, he saw that people were passing them thickly, making a wide eddy as they came near to the boy. They were eying him with a profound curiosity. He had passed beyond the ranks of ordinary mortals, in the opinions of those Indians. He had become a great medicine man, whose touch was sheer disaster to whoever was unlucky enough to feel it.

A thought had come to Lessing.

"Will you tell me how you got out of my room, this morning?" he asked.

"I unlocked the door, and walked out."

"You had no key."

"There are ways of opening locks without keys," said the boy, smiling a little. "I'm no great expert, but experts are not needed for simple locks like that one."

"Then do one thing for me."

"Lessing," said Messenger with feeling, "I'd do anything that I could for you!"

"Then go up and unlock that door and go into my room and sit there until I come up after you. Will you do that?"

The other hesitated only for a moment.

"I go now," he said, and made for the interior of the fort.

Lessing watched him go, and was still staring when a burly trader said at his shoulder: "Sleight of hand. That's what he's got! I never seen nothin' like it, and I was standin' as close as from me to you!"

"What did he do?" asked Lessing.

"It is a hard kind of a thing to tell you about. His hands, they moved as fast as a card sharp's. There's one heaves up a revolver over his head. I thought that the kid would have his brains bashed out. He reaches across as fast as a bird could flick a wing, and with the edge of his open hand—like this!—he chops Dan Vincent across the arm, close to the shoulder. You would've thought that Dan had been cut with an ax. He lets the gun drop and his arm falls to his side like it was paralyzed. And, while it's fallin', the kid shoves a fist into the pit of his stomach, and Dan drops onto the ground and begins kickin' and squirmin' to get back his wind. Casey Martin is takin' a free swing at the kid, and Messenger lets the punch fan over the top of his head, and he steps in then and smashes Martin in the middle of the face. You could hear the slug of it goin' home. Then Martin starts walkin' backward on his heels, and trips and goes flat. It was 'Home, Sweet Home' for Martin, I tell you. Jip Oliver, he seen enough and got going, but the kid pops him behind the ear, and it's as though he'd had a bullet go through his brain, right there. Down he goes on his face, and gives one shudder, and lies still."

"And what happened to Buck Chandler?" asked Lessing.

The other made a wry face, and his voice lowered to confidential tones.

"He had the gun wrung out of his hand," said the man, "and then his left arm was jerked around and twisted, slow, and sure, and easy, so's to linger out the pain for him—it was a sickenin' thing to see. You heard the arm pop, I reckon? I'll never get over the sound of it, if I live to be a hundred. I tell you, Messenger has a hand like iron."

"Aye," said Lessing, "he has a hand of iron!"

"Davis and Toomey Johnson will be packin' out of the fort pretty pronto," said the other. "They was on the firin' line when the kid was tossed in the blanket, last night. Think what a fellow he is. To let himself be throwed around like that, just to work up a good grudge, and all the time able to clean up that whole bunch like nothin' at all!"

Against this opinion of the superhuman prowess of the boy, Lessing did not argue. The fact that Messenger had had too much to drink would not have appeared reasonable to any man in the fort, accustomed as they were to the kicking powers of that so-called whisky. He merely said, now: "I tell you what. Go say to Toomey and Davis that they'd better stay tight in the fort. The kid don't know the faces or the names of the gents that throwed him. It was too dark for that. But tell them that the kid is likely to foller the trail of any man that pulls out of the fort sudden. He knows that he's throwed a scare into the boys, and he's likely to see which ones feels guilty."

The burly man started violently. "Aye!" he said. "I hadn't thought about that. I—I'll go tell the two of 'em."

And he went off with haunted eyes, like one who knows more than he cares to tell.

# 26

For his part, Lessing went straight to War Lance. And War Lance shook hands and gave the white man the smile which so perfectly softened his stern face.

"Come off here to a corner of the yard with me," said the trapper. "I have something to tell you, War Lance."

And he walked beside the chief to the edge of the yard, near the palisade.

Still, as he talked, War Lance kept his glance roving

among the crowd of his braves, and the women and children who filled up the interstices of the crowd. He knew how quickly a fight can start. A nudge, a word, a mere laugh might start knife play which only the thunder of his voice could stop.

Lessing began with care.

He took from his belt a little knife with a hilt inlaid with mother-of-pearl, in black and white, and at the butt of the hilt there was a big piece of red glass, cut into facets so that it glittered. The steel of the knife was poor. But the eye of the chief flashed when he saw the color of it.

"When I came across this, some time back," said the trapper, "I thought about you, War Lance, and I've carried it around with me till I'd have a chance to give it to you myself."

The chief received it with a deep breath of satisfaction.

"All my nation," said he, "knows that you are a friend. And what is better than to have for a friend such a warrior as Two Buffalo?"

The trapper swallowed a smile of pleasure, on his own part.

Long ago, a chance shot from his rifle, in running buffalo, had clipped the spinal column of one and dropped it dead, and ranging ahead, it had struck another cow to the heart. Two at one shot, and both of them young cows, in the prime for meat—that was a thing which the Indians would not attribute to chance! Lessing's name had been given to him upon the spot.

Now he said: "Who is luckier than the hunter who has the Blackfeet for friends? But all of the Blackfeet are not my friends, War Lance."

"Who among them," said the chief, "is an enemy of Two Buffalo?"

The trapper hesitated a moment, both to arrange un-

129

familiar words of the Blackfoot language, and also to make the most diplomatic approach possible to a delicate question.

"Sometimes," said he, "the wisest men are not the kindest."

"That is true," said War Lance, and nodded.

"Sometimes the strongest hand is not the most gentle one."

"Yes."

"Sometimes the greatest medicine man is easily made angry—when the spirits have made him nervous?"

War Lance looked straight into his face and said nothing. And the trapper saw that his diplomacy had been in vain. He came straight out with the next words, throwing all diplomacy aside.

"The great medicine man of the tribe, the great Summer Day, hates me, brother, and wants to take my hair and dry my scalp in his lodge."

War Lance, never stirring a feature of his face, continued to stare fixedly at the white man before him.

"Summer Day hates me," went on Lessing carefully, but honestly. "And I hate him. We get back from people what we give them."

"That is true," said War Lance, and the trapper was glad of the words. Anything was better than the critical silence of the big red man.

"Now, then," said Lessing, "when I go out into the mountains alone, it is not a good thing to remember that the great Summer Day is my enemy. I never ride over a hilltop without looking to see the face of the medicine man grow up on the other side, his rifle leveled at my breast."

The chief still waited impassively, listening.

"When the great Summer Day was here," said the trapper, "I wanted very much to make him my friend again. I am a humble man, brother. I am not one to keep up a hatred if I can buy my enemy off with words or with gifts. I would have given many horses and good rifles to Summer Day, if he would have become my friend again, as he was before."

"Was he once your friend?" said the chief.

"He was. There was a matter of trading between us, and the rifle he got from me burst in his hands—because he overcharged it. But he always felt that I had bewitched the gun!"

The other nodded.

"And then," said the trapper, "there came the battle between Summer Day and my young white friend—"

He paused. There was no Indian name for the boy, as yet. And the word "Messenger" would hardly make any meaning in the Blackfoot tongue.

"The young brave with the iron hand, the 'Iron Hand' is your friend?" said the chief.

Thereby, Messenger had his name given to him, and by no small authority.

"That's it," nodded the trapper. "The Iron Hand goes out to fight with Summer Day, and comes back, and Summer Day says that he has won the fight, and at the same time, the spirits tell him to move camp and go seven days to the west!"

He stopped. War Lance, with unfailing presence, met the inquiring eye of the white man, and Lessing repeated the idea, more slowly:

"It was a strange battle. Many things about it were strange—to be told and hardly believed. We know, now, what a great warrior the Iron Hand is. We have seen him take men and break them like twigs."

"It is true," nodded the chief. "I have seen it with my own eyes."

"I will tell you other strange things," said the trapper. "Summer Day conquered this great fighter, but he did not

131

take his scalp. Although without mercy, yet he showed mercy to the white man. Although Summer Day is a great singer, yet after this battle he made no song. He did not stop to dance about the fire. He did not stop to tell the coup. He had too many spirits talking in his ears and telling him to go west as fast as he could go. Is it true?"

The war chief frowned. "It is true," he said doubtfully.

"Summer Day won the great fight there in the woods. The white man, however, had a strange dream. He dreamed that he won the fight, and that he almost throttled Summer Day, and that Summer Day, to get away from the Iron Hand, threw himself over the edge of the cliff, and slid down, and the Iron Hand thought the Blackfoot had fallen into the river and been torn to pieces among the rocks. Then he dreamed that he sat down to rest, and finally, he went to get the horse of Summer Day, and ride it around to pick up his own horse—but he found that it was all a dream, and Summer Day had galloped away on my horse and gone home shouting about a great victory—and about voices of the spirits that ordered the whole tribe to go west, seven days."

War Lance looked earnestly into the face of the other.

"If the Iron Hand ever was on the throat of the medicine man, then there are marks of the finger tips!" he said.

"There are!" said the trapper. "Of course there are! And big marks, I'd take it. Yes, sir, big marks, War Lance, and you'll find that Summer Day has taken to wearing something or other around his neck to keep it warm, or to make the spirits happy!"

War Lance frowned. He said, rather tersely: "What made you tell me—about this dream, my friend?"

The trapper threw his last card upon the table, face up.

"Because you hate Summer Day," he said, "and because you know that he is a cheat and a sayer of that which is not true!"

132

The blow was so sudden, and so unexpected, that War Lance wavered backward a little. He recovered himself at once and drew himself up to his full height.

"Think a minute," said the white man soberly. "If I am not wrong, you are going to get a treasure from me, War Lance!"

Suddenly the war chief broke out, though struggling with his voice: "Summer Day is a great chief among the Blackfeet. I have not said that he is my friend!"

"Very well," said the trapper. "If he's a liar and a cheat, you don't want that sort of a man making false medicine among the Blackfeet and giving them wrong medicine to take with them on the warpath.

"What has he done for you? Has he ever gone with a great war party and had a great victory? No, he hunts like a buzzard. He prefers dead things! But War Lance goes out and wins great battles, and comes home covered with scars! Now, then, my friend, listen to me! The Iron Hand has not forgotten the medicine man. He wishes to see him again. He wishes to stand in a Blackfoot tepee, where there are many chiefs standing around, and he wishes to say: 'This medicine man, this great and famous Summer Day, he is no more than a liar and a thief. He told a lie and counted a coup which he had no right to count. Therefore, he is no more a medicine man than a barking dog. Let him admit that this is true, or else let him fight with me again, not in the woods, but in the open plain, where every man can see and judge the truth!' That is what the Iron Hand wants to do. Will you, War Lance, take him with you?"

The breast of the chief expanded in a great breath. He looked fiercely to the right, and then to the left.

"If he comes with me," said War Lance, "it may be said that I have taken the enemies of the Blackfeet into my lodge and given them comfort, like a friend!"

"He is no enemy to any man," said the trapper, "except

the ones who injure him; but to every man that lays the weight of a finger on him, he'll not hesitate to lay the weight of iron on his heart in return!"

The chief smiled suddenly.

"It is a good fault," said he. "May my own sons have such a fault, Two Buffalo!"

"Let him go with you, then. Take him as soon as the day's trading is finished. Take him away, and let him have a chance, as soon as the time comes, to stand face to face with Summer Day. It will do you no harm. It is a good thing for every tribe to know where the liars sit, and throw them out of the circle of the brave men!"

War Lance suddenly gripped his hand with all his might.

The force made the fingers of the trapper crumble together, giving great pain, but he smiled, and gave no token.

"Send the young man to me," said the chief.

"I go to find him," said the trapper, and went off with a lightness in his step, for he knew that he had crossed a very long bridge indeed—if only he could persuade the boy to go with him.

# 27

For two days young Messenger hesitated. It was true that there seemed no other logical way of coming at Summer Day, if he should fail to join the band of War Lance. If he went out by himself on a solitary trail, he would be passing alone into a country swarming with hundreds of red men; and though he might outmatch almost any three of them in single combat, there was hardly a brave in the entire tribe who was not capable of outmaneuvering him and lifting his scalp with ease.

On the third day, he agreed with the trapper that there was nothing else for it. And, together, they rode out in the evening to the camp of the war chief.

The trading of the latter's party had by this time been completed. They had given in their robes and other articles of commercial value, and they had received in exchange the ammunition, guns, knives, and trinkets of the fort. Now under the strict leadership of War Lance, they had to prepare to depart at once.

In the dusk of the evening, they came to the camp, when the western sky was bordered with crimson, and pale green above, verging into the deeper blue of the upper heavens. As they came closer, two braves appeared, as it were, from nowhere, and rode toward them.

"Don't be worried by 'em," explained the trapper. "You take most Injun camps, and they don't bother about sentinels and mounting guard. They trust to luck, mostly, and take their chances. They've got eyes as sharp as the eyes of lynxes, of course. But a lynx can catch a lynx, and War Lance knows it. Nobody's ever surprised one of his camps. He's never lost so much as a single hoss by the stealin' of Crows, or Sioux, or any of the rest of 'em. These two gents, they'll ask a few questions, and take us into the camp."

That was exactly what happened.

When the braves came near, they called out to know who was there, and when they heard the names, they immediately formed up beside the white men and accompanied them into the center of the camp. They seemed sufficiently proud of their mission, at that. When children and dogs scampered across the lane down which they were riding, one or the other of them would call out, saying: "Out of our way! Are you going to make the horses of chiefs and warriors fall over you? Out of the way, and let two white braves come into our camp—Two Buffalo, and the Iron Hand!"

It was clear that the second name was to the youngsters like an explosion of gunpowder. They yipped like young coyotes when they heard it, and while some swarmed close alongside the younger of the white men, others scampered ahead, and roused the lodges along the way.

Then the flaps of tepees were thrown aside; squaws and old men stepped into the entrances; and young Messenger, as he went past, had glimpses of fires twinkling and smoking in the interiors of the lodges, and he saw the glitter of beadwork and weapons. A pungent odor breathed from the whole camp. There was the taint of wood smoke, and the smell of unfamiliar foods cooking; and by the sense of smell more than anything else he recognized that he had passed into quite another world.

It seemed as if all the life in the camp was rushing to view him. An uproar began like the noise of a sea.

As they came to the center of the camp, the guides took them at once toward the largest tepee in the last circle of lodges. Before it stood a lofty form which the boy recognized easily, even through the dusk, as the great War Lance, himself.

They came up to him and dismounted, the trapper holding up his right hand as he said: "How!"

This example the boy imitated, and the chief returned the greeting.

"I've brought him in as I promised," said the trapper. "It's for you to hold him if you can, War Lance."

The latter replied: "Come into my lodge. There we can talk."

He threw aside the flap of the lodge, and into it they

136

passed. A low fire burned in the center, with the usual big iron pot hanging above it. On her knees at one side of the tepee, a woman was busily sharpening a knife with a very long blade, and near her a baby of two years rolled with a toy. It got up on its chubby legs, and the mother rose also. She still had some of the light grace of body which distinguishes Indian girls, but her hands were big from labor and her face was not beautiful. She had a big, intelligent eye, but certainly War Lance was not above the ordinary taste of his nation when it came to picking out a wife for himself.

The two white men were seated on either hand of the host just opposite the entrance to the lodge, which was the place of honor. Reclining there against very comfortable back rests, they were offered food, which they barely tasted, and which the boy found tasteless because of the lack of salt in the cookery. Next they accepted the pipe, which was lighted by the chief, who blew smoke to the spirits of the air, and to the underground people.

After these preliminaries, it was possible to talk seriously. The trapper was the go-between.

"The Iron Hand," said he, "because I see that name has been given to my friend by your people, will come to you, War Lance, and be one of your men. He only asks that while he fights for you in your battles, he shall be allowed to live his own life as it pleases him. And when he finds the man you know of, his hands shall be free!"

"The Iron Hand," said the chief, addressing the trapper, "is a great brave, as all the Blackfeet know. It may be that the medicine man put a spell on him and made him dream a strange dream. But the affairs of Summer Day are not my affairs. He has the Sky People to talk with him and to advise him from time to time. They can protect him from all dangers, as he often has said. All that I wish to know is that the Iron Hand will be a warrior in this tribe, and that he will swear not to leave it for one great sun."

"A year!" exclaimed the trapper. "You want him to promise to live with you for a whole year?"

"Yes. Unless something happens in the meantime that forces him to flee for his life from the revenge of the Blackfeet!"

The boy nodded. "I understand," said he.

"And if ever you lift a hand against a member of the Blackfoot tribe," went on War Lance sternly, "it must be because you have seen good proofs that the man is a criminal, and that you will be able to show those proofs to all the nation."

"Hold on," said Messenger to the trapper. "He wants me to promise what I'll probably not be able to do."

"If you challenged the medicine man to a fair fight and he was beaten by you, they'd take that as proof that his medicine was no good and that he was a liar and had lied about the first fight that he had with you."

Young Messenger nodded. "That seems better," said he.

"Will you make the promise?"

"Why does he want me for a whole year?"

"Because," said War Lance, "if you stay with us a month, you would then leave us forever. If you stay with us a year, you may never wish to change."

Messenger looked quickly around at the eathern floor of the tepee, the steaming meat pot, the awkward paintings on the wall, and though he did not smile, he could not help shrugging.

But the trapper took the thing more seriously.

"He may be right. Will you do it, Messenger? You'll get the taste of this life, before long, just as you'll learn to like that sort of boiled meat a lot better than anything that the French chefs can serve up to you."

"I go with him," said Messenger softly, to himself, "or else I never reach Summer Day. So go with him I must.

War Lance, I will stay with you a year, and injure no Blackfoot except to protect myself, or because I have proof that he is a guilty man in the eyes of your people. Is that enough?"

"No," said the chief. "It is not enough."

He went to a corner of the lodge and took down a bridle from a whole cluster of them that hung from a peg.

"I have eight friends," he said, "who ride with me. Sometimes they ride hunting by themselves, and then they use their own bridles and their own horses. But when they ride with me, they use my horses, and they ride with these bridles. Will the Iron Hand do as they do? Will he be one of the companions?"

The trapper started.

"Did you see it?" he said aside to the boy. "He's asking you to join up with that sacred band of his. He's making you the ninth man in the lot, and that's enough to set the whole tribe by the ears, because there never have been more than eight of them before."

The eyes of Messenger glittered. He had not forgotten those eight splendid warriors who had ridden past him at the gate of the fort.

"Yes," said he.

The chief reached one side of the bridle toward him, and retained the other in his own grasp. Then he raised his right hand above his head and looked upward.

"Iron Hand," said he, "from this moment my lodge is your lodge, my food is your food, my weapons are your weapons, my horse is your horse, and my life is your life, brother!"

He spoke with a solemn emotion, and the boy looked on him as though hearing the voice of a ghost. His eyes widened. And suddenly he repeated in a tone which was uncertain at first, but which rose and rang toward the end:

"War Lance, from this moment my lodge is your lodge, my food is your food, my weapons are your weapons, my horse is your horse, and my life is your life, brother!"

The trapper looked on agape. He could not tell exactly what had happened, but he guessed that a spirit miraculously strong had touched the soul of Messenger, and strange things might be the spiritual fruit of it.

# 28

Now that the trading was ended and that the tribe was to start on the following morning, Lessing decided that he would accompany them. His chief reason, as he admitted to himself, was that he wished to be in touch with the further adventures of young Messenger. Messenger himself he left in the camp of the Blackfeet, where hospitality was offered him in the lodge of the chief. And Lessing went back to wind up his affairs at the fort, prepare his pack, and start off, early the following morning, to join the Blackfeet.

He was busied until well into the night in arranging his pack of traps, and other essentials. He had bought a small but strong mule to carry most of the pack, and the Indian pony which had once belonged to Summer Day would carry the rest of the pack and the trapper himself.

He was in bed late, but he was up when the dawn was still a pale pink, and life had hardly begun to stir in the fort. It was high time, however, to set out after the Blackfeet, for they would be early on the march. Perhaps already they were streaming away through the woods and over the hills!

Two things delayed and infuriated Lessing. First, the Indian pony bucked off saddle, pack, Lessing and all. When he had been resaddled, and a precious half hour or so had been wasted, the mule, tired of the chill of the morning, refused to budge. Nothing would urge him out of his tracks until the sun was well up and beginning to warm the air.

And then, just as Lessing was about to make a belated start, a third interruption made him grit his teeth. For up to the fort came a new party. There was a half-breed guide, and two sturdy frontiersmen who had been manning paddles or pull ropes all the way up the river, and in addition to these, there was a man with as strange a personality as ever had come to Fort Lippewan.

No sooner had this stranger arrived than he asked questions which caused a messenger to run over to Lessing.

He was wanted because the stranger was inquiring for a young man of the exact description of Messenger.

Lessing was on the verge of refusing. He had halted far too long, already, but curiosity checked him for a little while. He remained there while the stranger came up to him, with his two big canoeman flanking him on either side, and a little behind. Lessing well knew what that attitude meant. They were getting wages so high that they were willing to play the subservient role of domestic servants, even.

As for the man himself, he was, perhaps, forty-five or fifty. It seemed apparent that he had just recovered from an illness, and that he was about to sink again—it was hard to make any other explanation of the hollowness of his chest, and the extreme emaciation of his face. His leanness was exaggerated by the hawklike cast of his features, but there was one thing about him that most attracted the attention of the trapper, and that was his eye. For it was the color and brilliance of iron, newly broken, and glittering in the sunlight. Lessing knew that he had seen that eye before.

"You're the man who knows the young fellow?" asked the stranger.

"Messenger, you mean?"

"Messenger?" said the stranger. "Yes, that's the name."

But he gave the trapper a strong suggestion of hearing the name for the first time at that moment.

"I mean," said the stranger, continuing, "a tall, rather slender young fellow, with gray eyes, and the general appearance—"

He paused, not as one in doubt, but rather as one anxious to pick out the most accurate word.

"General appearance of a cat?" suggested the trapper.

The stranger did not smile. Yet he seemed to accept the description as identifying Messenger once for all.

"They tell me that you know where he has gone?"

"I do."

"Where is he, then?"

"Stranger," said Lessing. "I know Messenger pretty well, but I never seen you before, and I dunno why you're on his trail."

This bluntness did not offend the other. He merely said: "My name is Thomas Vance. I've come a good part of two thousand miles to see that young man. You'll help me to find him, I hope?"

"He's gone off with the Blackfeet," said the trapper.

"With the Blackfeet?" said the other. "He's gone off *with* the Blackfeet, did you say?"

And his eyes literally shot fire as he spoke.

"He's gone off with them. He's made friends with War Lance."

"War Lance? Who is he?"

"The biggest chief among the tribe, and the biggest power, next to Summer Day, the medicine man."

"Where have they gone?" snapped Thomas Vance.

"West, I reckon."

Vance struck his hands together and took two or three excited steps up and down. Then he turned again to Lessing.

"Your name is what?"

"Lessing."

"Lessing. I see you're about to travel. Are you going in his direction, by any chance?"

"I might be," said the trapper, noncommittally.

"If you will, I'll pay you well for it. I would go on myself, but I'm worn out. I want you to take a letter to young Messenger. One of these men of mine will go along with you and bring back his answer."

"Hold on," said one of the canoemen. "I know them Blackfeet, and they know me, and the only use that they'd have for me would be to toast me on one of their fires. I'll keep clean of them, thanks. They'd be wearin' my hair five minutes after I got into their camp."

"How about you, Bray?" snapped Vance, looking at the other big frontiersman.

The latter was the younger and the bigger of the two.

"Waal, I dunno," he remarked. "They've gone and got themselves the scalps of my pa, and Uncle Henry Wales, and my cousins, the two Wales boys. But we've kind of evened up on our side. I've lifted the hair of three-four of them myself. I dunno why I should give 'em a chance to play the game with a cold pack, at my expense!"

Said the traveler dryly, coldly: "I'll give you a hundred dollars if you take this message, and from Messenger back to the fort."

The canoeman shook his head.

"It's a pile of money," he admitted. "It's a hundred beaver pelts all in a heap—but, a hundred dollars don't do no good to a dead man, so far as I ever have heard!"

"Bray," said Vance, without the slightest emotion. "I'll give you a hundred and fifty dollars!"

"Hold on!" said a bystander. "I'll go for that. I'll go for the hundred, for that matter!"

Vance hardly looked at the profferer.

"I know this man, and not you!" he answered in his crisp way.

Bray took off his hat and ran his fingers through his hair.

"A hundred and fifty is a hundred and fifty," he announced wisely. "And I reckon that I'll have to die some day, no matter what. Hey, Lessing, you're a friend of the Blackfeet, you might help me out with 'em!"

"I think that I can," said the trapper, "but no man is ever sure of a red Injun, unless he's a sworn blood brother to one of 'em!"

"Aye," said the canoeman, "and that's true, but I reckon that I'll take this job. Where's the letter, Mr. Vance?"

"Here. And here's the money."

"Leave the money with Louis Desparr. If they get me, it'll be a comfort to think that they didn't get the coin with me. Where's the letter?"

"Here," said Thomas Vance.

He opened a wallet and from an inner fold he took out an envelope which carried, as the close eye of the trapper saw, a foreign stamp—two of them, in fact. And the face of the envelope was soiled and covered with much writing and rewriting of addresses. This Vance wrapped with much caution in a piece of oiled silk that went several times around it. He tied the package with a string, and gave it to Bray.

"Bray," he said, "I'll do better than I said. I'll give you two hundred and fifty dollars—gold! And I'll add two hundred and fifty more if you'll bring back his answer safely to this fort."

Money was not easily come by in those days and five hundred dollars in gold was a sum that made the eyes of Bray pop from his head.

"For five hundred dollars," he said, "I can dodge bullets and jump through mountains. I'm gunna bring back that letter to you, all right!"

Vance, for the first time pleased, smiled. It was only a shadow of a smile, cold as the light in his eyes, and both reminded the trapper forcibly of the smile and the cold eye of young Messenger.

There was now still another delay while Bray secured a horse, for which the inexhaustible purse of Vance paid without question; but inside of an hour, Bray's small pack was lashed firmly behind the saddle, and off he went in company with Lessing.

# 29

For half the day the conversation of Lessing and his companion was limited to the following remarks: "Kind of strong, the Lippewan is running," said the trapper, after they had been two hours on the way.

"Kind of dang strong," said big young Mr. Bray.

At about noon, as they were trudging along a narrow pass between hills whose sides were strewn with boulders, big and small: "Hot," said young Mr. Bray.

"Hot," agreed the trapper.

Though they spoke seldom, they were not unaware of

one another. Each examined, covertly but with a religious interest, the way the other's pack had been built and bound on, and how his saddle was placed on the horse's back and the horse itself, and the clothes and the weapons of the stranger.

Well on in the early part of the afternoon, they came to a place under some big trees beside a stream of running water, and there they halted without asking one another's opinion.

This unanimity of silent opinion pleased them both.

Finally, as being the older of the two, the trapper took it upon him to break the ice.

"You've been in the mountains before," he suggested.

"I reckon you was *born* in the mountains," answered Bray.

Suddenly a wall fell down between them. It was invisible, and its fall made no sound; but both of them knew that it had stood there stronger than steel; and now they knew that it was gone.

They did not divide tasks in preparing for that noon meal.

As the older man, Lessing simply rigged up an improvised fishing line and went out on the edge of the rocks, where he sat with a humped back and fished. The younger man, without a word of doubt or of challenge, did all the serious labor of removing the packs and saddles from the backs of the animals, and hobbling them in a good grassy meadow nearby. Then he, with a small hand ax, cut up a quantity of brush, and laid and kindled a fire.

By the time it was going, old Lessing came casually back with half a dozen good-sized fish. These he cleaned with the expedition of one who knows how to work with a fast knife for a hungry stomach. He wrapped the fish first in some herbs which grew nearby, and then in broader leaves, and putting the fish in a pile, covered with dust and ashes, in the center of the fire, he piled the brush around it and made it burn fiercely.

In a few moments, however, so thoroughly had the cooking been done that the skin flaked away at a touch, and the flesh came away from the bones. Bray ate ravenously, and when he had finished his share, he took without a word the extra fish which the trapper did not want to complete his portion.

By this time, when the meal was done, they lighted their pipes. Up to this point, neither of them had spoken during the meal.

Then Lessing allowed himself to speak of the thing which was eating his very heart for curiosity.

"That Thomas Vance—" he slowly began.

"Yeah, that Vance," said the younger man. "Yeah!"

"You wouldn't see many—"

"No, you bet you wouldn't see many." Then Bray added eloquently: "He's made of money, just about!"

"Well," said Lessing, "I'd sure like to know—"

Again his voice trailed away. He seemed to be fighting against his hunger for gossip.

And Bray, after watching him for a time, almost wistfully, broke out: "He ain't out here for no good!"

"I'd lay my money that he ain't," said the other. He never said nothin'?"

"No, not a word about nothin', except Blackfeet. He's pretty curious about 'em. Maybe he's gunna write one of them fool books."

The trapper shook his head.

"Whatever he does, it won't be foolish."

"Well, he's deep," said Bray.

"Yeah, he's deep."

The pipes being finished, they resaddled the horses and

the pack mule, and mounted. But, when they resumed their way, instead of riding one behind the other, they rode abreast, where the windings of the narrow trail permitted. Before them, now, they had innumerable signs of the Indians who had preceded them, not only in the long, snaky marks of the travois poles, but also other signs—a worn-out moccasin, for instance.

They could tell that the band was not very far ahead, and, therefore, they did not urge their animals strictly. If there was any likelihood of trouble between Bray and the Blackfeet, it would be far wiser to come upon the band at night, when the tired warriors, after the day's ride, would have less mischief than weariness in their minds.

"This fellow, Messenger," said Bray. "Tell me, just what's he like?"

"I dunno," said the trapper. "He's a friend of mine. I've known him one day," he added, with a soft chuckle, "but I've seen a good deal of him. A couple days is all that I've known him."

"He ain't like nothin'?" asked the other, pointblank.

"I wouldn't say that he's like nothin'. Except a sort of a cat."

"Why, that's what old Vance is like, too," said Bray, surprised.

"Yeah. They're something alike. You'll see. They got some of the same blood in them, I reckon!"

As he said it, surety came upon the trapper. Who Messenger was, from what place he had come, why he had been sent out to the West on an errand of blood revenge, who had trained him to his present physical perfection—those all seemed questions which might be answered by something that was to come to pass between Vance and the boy.

They had bad luck, later on in the afternoon.

For they came to a strong young river that rushed and roared through a narrow valley. At the place where it was narrowest, the Indians had felled all of the trees near the bank, and over this natural bridge they had taken their way. Then, once across on the farther side, they had tumbled the logs into the stream and gone on their way. For Indians like to leave a broken trail behind them even in the most peaceful times.

This was a great stroke of bad fortune for the two who pursued that trail.

They had to work up the stream several miles before they came to a place where it could be crossed, though with some danger and difficulty.

Night was close on them when they reached the farther side. So they camped, and the next day had to return downstream to the point where they had lost the trail the night before.

This was a serious loss.

For five days longer they pushed on behind the party of Blackfeet, for on the third day their march had been again interrupted in an exactly similar manner. But, on the fifth day, they came at evenfall upon sight of a small hollow, spotted with the white-glowing tepees of the Indians, and down toward them they went, glad that their long pursuit was over.

Bray, with the calm of a brave man, showed not the slightest nervousness, but he allowed the trapper to do the talking when they came into the camp and were encountered by the mounted scouts.

They, at the name of Two Buffalo, showed every sign of pleasure. As for Bray, he was not regarded, because his face could not be seen in the dark of the evening. And so the pair were conducted straight to the tepee of the chief.

War Lance was not there. The squaw was busy weaving a

willow bed with great care and skill; the child was asleep on a robe; and in a corner, stretched against a slanted back rest, his hands behind his head, and his eyes turned up to watch the flight of the smoke through the vent at the top of the lodge, was Messenger at last.

# 30

When the boy saw his friend, he leaped suddenly to his feet and seized his hand. No matter how indifferent he might be to the rest of the world, he had opened the door of his heart to the old trapper, and the face of the latter glowed when he recognized the joy in the eyes of the boy.

They must sit down. They must eat, and they must smoke. Gladly they did so, and the squaw served them from the meat pot, where there was fresh meat stewing, for the hunt had been very successful this day. They ate gluttonously, and then, as they sat back to smoke, the letter was given to the boy.

He unwrapped it with a frown, but at the sight of the postmark upon the outside of it, he started. And then, scrutinizing the handwriting carefully, they saw him bound to his feet. He turned white. Then, opening the letter, old Lessing marveled to see the iron hand was shaking. Once or twice the boy lowered the letter with a sick look. But he read on, and when the letter was finished, he went patiently through it, again and again.

A sudden fury made him crush the paper and hurl it in

the fire. But a reaction sent him leaping after it faster than the stroke of a snake. After this, he remained for a long moment holding the missive in both his hands, with the look of a man who is finishing a long-distance race.

Finally, recovering himself a little, he rewrapped the letter in the oiled silk with the same care which Thomas Vance had shown for it, and placed it carefully in his wallet.

Lessing was more amazed than if the ground had opened at his feet. He would have ventured his life that there was nothing in the world that could so shake the nerve of that young creature of steel and rock. Bray, in the meantime, was looking askance at these exhibitions of emotion.

Once the letter was put away, the boy recalled himself. He began to show more attention to his guests, asking them about their journey, and Bray put the matter bluntly.

"I didn't come out here to do you a favor, man. I come here to earn five hundred dollars that that Vance offered, and I want to get out of here with your answer to him, as fast as I can get, before these red men get a chance to recognize me. There's bad blood between the tribe and me, Messenger!"

"My answer back to him?" exclaimed the youngster, turning as crimson as he had been white before. "Go back and tell him—tell him—"

He checked himself, and they saw his hands working.

"He'll have to wait for his answer," said Messenger at last, almost sullenly. "He knew that. You'll have to stay with us a while if you want to get the message back to him. Didn't he tell you that you would?"

"No, he told me nothin' about it. Only, I was to take back your answer to him. Messenger, whatever the answer is, I gotta have it now. I ain't scary. But I got a little common sense."

"You're afraid of these fellows?" said Messenger, waving his hand. "They won't touch you. Not a man of them would

151

dare to touch you, Bray. You're in the lodge of War Lance. That's enough. If it weren't, you're my friend. You came here to see me. And that's enough to keep their hands off you."

Bray, in spite of himself, eyed the boy and sneered faintly.

"I dunno how thick a shield of bull's hide you're holdin' over me, Messenger," he said, "but I know how straight Blackfoot bullets can fly and what they'll cut through!"

The suggested doubt did not trouble Messenger. He replied quietly that everything would be well with Bray. He would pledge his honor for that. War Lance, at that moment, came in. He greeted the trapper gravely but kindly. On Bray he turned with a cold and still eye.

Said Messenger: "This man, War Lance, came to me as a friend. He traveled for a week to bring me a message. Is he safe here with you and the rest of the braves?"

War Lance paused a moment before he replied: "This man has been an enemy, but he has been a brave enemy. We are willing to have him with us, and every man in the tribe will be his friend so long as he cares to stay. When he leaves us, every many will try again to count coup on him. For there is more honor," said the chief, "in counting one coup on a brave man than in counting fifty on cowards."

After this speech, which Bray followed fairly well, the canoeman was much relieved, and he said to young Messenger: "Once they've passed their word, no man will be harmed by 'em. And I'll trust to luck. You can't tell me how long I'll be waiting here for your answer, Messenger?"

The latter shook his head.

Preparations were next made for the sleeping quarters of the two white men who had just arrived, and they were given beds in the lodge of War Lance himself. Because, as he said, the young men of the tribe were a turbulent lot, and it was better to have Bray under his own protection. As for Two Buffalo, he was an old and valued friend.

So they turned in for the night, with the fire flickering low in the center of the lodge, and the shadows leaping and falling upon the hide walls. For an Indian night, it was comparatively quiet. Only, now and again, a wave of wolfish howling and snarling swept the encampment as a tangle of dogs started fighting.

But to men tired out by a long march, such disturbances were hardly enough to make them open their eyes. The sounds which began with the dawn were of an entirely different nature.

For then one could hear the young men shooting as they ran down in groups for the early-morning plunge which, winter and summer, marked the beginning of the day for them. The dogs started yipping in higher key. Horses neighed and answered one another.

Bray and the trapper wandered out to the edge of the camp and there they could see the flashing curve of the little stream, rosy in the morning light. Sounds of shouting and laughter came up from it, and presently, over the edge of the bank which hid the place where the swimmers were bathing, there flashed a line of twenty young warriors, naked except for breechclouts, and racing desperately for the camp. They carried their clothes under their arms; their half-dried bodies, from which the water had merely been whipped with the edge of the hand, glistened brightly as they flew over the ground. But on one figure of that racing line the two watchers fastened their eyes.

This was one who was made slenderly, except about the shoulders, and his body flashed a pure, dazzling white.

"Messenger!" exclaimed the watchers, with one voice.

"Somebody else watching," said Bray, and gestured aside. "And white, too, by jumping Jimmy!"

The trapper glanced in the indicated direction and saw a picture which startled him. It was a girl who was perfect Indian in her clothes, and with a face sun-browned almost to the coppery darkness of the Indian skin. But the hair which was drawn over her shoulders was shining gold.

She, with clasped hand and glistening eyes of pleasure, watched the race sweep toward the village. Others came running from lodges, women, older warriors, children. They set up a shout, for now the line grew ragged. It bowed out in the center, and here, side by side, appeared a pair of racers who were evenly matched. One was a Blackfoot, straining every nerve and his face ugly even in the distance with effort. The other was the slender, gleaming body of the white boy. And, though he matched the Indian stride for stride, he seemed to be running without a great effort.

Fifty yards from the camp they were shoulder to shoulder, but here it seemed as though Messenger leaned forward a little. His stride increased. He leaped away like a greyhound unleashed and shot into the camp by himself.

A tremendous and cordial shout went up from all who watched the contest. But the trapper, regardless of the victor, regardless of all the others who were whooping, kept his eyes fixed fast upon the white girl—or was she a half-breed?

She had not turned to stare after the victor. Neither did she regard the other runners, but with her hands clasped together, she was looking toward the brightness of the eastern sky.

"Trouble!" growled Lessing to himself. "Trouble ahead for her, poor girl!"

# 31

They found out about the girl easily.

She was Yellow Antelope, the daughter of Rolling Thunder, a good brave now considerably past his prime. She was as white as her skin, it appeared, for she had been taken from white people, not on a raid, but from the stricken camp of a poor emigrant whose wife already had died of the terrible spotted disease, and who himself was on the point of death. They had with them this one child, and because the tepee of Rolling Thunder was totally without children, his heart had been touched by the little one. So he had taken her, apparently untainted by the disease. He had given her a name suggested by her young grace and the color of her hair, and adopted her into his family. The war party which was with him, dreading the mortal sickness, had refused to allow him to ride with it. And he had gone alone across a considerable district, caring for the little one, holding it in the saddle on his war pony, while he walked beside and led the horse. From that time on he had doted on her; and this adoption, this whole achievement of the long march through enemy's country, was looked upon by the tribe as the most honorable exploit of the brave.

An old woman gave this information to Lessing.

"There is a girl of eighteen or nineteen," said the trapper, "and that is four or five past the time when most of your girls are taken as wives. Will none of the warriors have her?"

"Friend," said the woman, "in these last years, twenty of

155

our best warriors have tied their finest horses outside of the lodge of Rolling Thunder. But she is not to be sold until she finds a man who pleases both her and her father. Well, that is a foolish thing. If matters had been handled in a better way, she might now be a mother with two or three children about her, and some chief would be made happy to have her. But a man with one daughter is like a hunter with one bullet. He is never ready to spend it."

Lessing discovered that it was not the first time that the boy had distinguished himself in a minor way since he started with the tribe toward the west on the long six-day march. He was the perfect picture of a rising brave, and War Lance was considered to have done well by himself and all his people in adding such a champion to the list of his chosen fighters.

Lessing had a chance to talk to Messenger later on in the day. He had gone down to fish, and he found that the boy was already there by the bank of the stream, not fishing, but musing over the sun and shadow that rippled upon the bottom of the shallow creek. For there was no march this day—War Lance intended to make a halt here to extend over a considerable period. Lessing made ready his fishing gear. The boy helped him to untangle the line.

"You're getting sunburned, Messenger," said the trapper. The boy nodded.

"And you've got a few of the wrinkles out of your forehead, too!"

Messenger lifted his hand and touched the fingertips across his forehead. Still he did not speak.

"You came out expecting to find it hell," suggested the trapper suddenly, "and at least, it ain't been that."

At this, Messenger smiled faintly.

"No," he answered quietly. "It's been almost the reverse." He added, with the look of one fumbling in his mind: "There's nothing shadowy about these Indians, Lessing."

"What d'you mean by 'shadowy'?"

"I mean that white men—they're always showing only half a face to one. They're more slippery than fish. But the Indian—you know how to take hold on him."

"You've been wrestling with some of the braves, then, I reckon?" said the trapper.

"A little," nodded the boy. "They're strong, but they haven't been trained. But they don't bear any malice. There was one fellow—his name is Bear-that-wakened-in-the-middle-of-the-night, or some such thing. He was proud of his wrestling. I put him down softly, three times; but he came dancing back for more, and finally I had to throw him hard. It whacked the wind out of him. He got up and grinned at me. What do you think he said?"

"That he'd wear your scalp, someday?"

"He said: 'Fire burns four times for a child; once for a wise man.' And ever since that time, we've been great friends."

"I thought that you'd be kind of lost, out here in the wilds," suggested the trapper.

"Not when I have men like that along with me. They're real. They're so real that the rest of my life seems smoky and half lost already."

"What's going to happen about the medicine man, Messenger?"

"The medicine man? Oh, War Lance sent a message to him three days ago, by a fast-riding young brave who went ahead and ought to be back with a reply, today."

"What was the message?"

"War Lance sent it from himself. He said that he had a new warrior who had joined his party—they call me the Iron Hand, do you see?"

"I know that. He said that the Iron Hand was with him. What then?"

"He said that I swear the account that Summer Day gave of the fight was a thing not true—they don't seem to have a word for 'lie'."

"No, they haven't."

"The result is that I am supposed to say that Summer Day has weak medicine, says the thing that is not so, and has counted a coup which is not a fact. I am willing to support what I say by a fight in the open, or in the woods, or anywhere that Summer Day says; but I prefer to have it in front of the braves of both the parties, if possible."

"That why War Lance camped here—to get the answer?"

"No. There's been a whisper in the air, it seems, that there's a big band of Crows trailing up through the mountains and ready to eat us up. War Lance has a couple of men scouting to the east, and he's waiting here to get more definite news. If they're behind us, I daresay that he'll try to do some of the eating himself."

"Well," said Lessing gravely, "I never expected it, but it looks like you're pretty fond of the Blackfeet. Lemme warn you about one thing. Would you listen?"

"Certainly," said the boy.

"It's this. A lot of the whites think that the Injuns are plain beasts, which they ain't. And when they find out, all of a sudden, that the red men are about as straight as the whites, and in their own way just as honorable, then sometimes they go to the other extreme, and the first thing they know, they wake up one day and find out that they've married some Injun girl."

Messenger raised his head a little, but he said nothing. His bright, hard, gray eyes looked fixedly at the trapper.

"But the time comes," said Lessing, "when every man is a lot better off with his own kind. And though sometimes you find a white girl living with the Injuns, it don't matter.

The color of the skin don't count, if she's been raised in the Injun ways of things."

"Why d'you say that to me?" asked the boy.

"Because," said the trapper, "when you was runnin' that race this morning, I noticed that Yellow Antelope sure was lookin' at you, and I reckon that you've looked at her, too!"

Messenger half rose, but by an apparent effort of the will, he forced himself to sit down again.

"You think that she has noticed me?" he said. His eyes were shining very brightly.

Lessing bit his lip.

"Maybe I've talked like a fool. But remember what I've warned you, son. This here wild free life, it can go to the head of a man quicker than whisky."

"I hope not," said the boy, more gravely than before.

They remained silent for a moment, but there was a speculative and contented light in the eye of young Messenger that made the trapper curse his clumsiness of speech. It occurred to him that in attempting to prevent the growth of an idea, he actually had planted the first seed of it.

And just then another man joined them, a stalwart brave well upward of six feet in height and with the look of a hero.

"Brother," said he to the boy, "War Lance wishes to speak with you."

Lessing, watching, saw the head of Messenger lift, and the first thoroughly gentle smile he ever had seen appeared on the mouth of the boy. Patently, he and this big warrior were sworn friends.

"It is Waking Bear, as we call him for short," explained Messenger. "I come at once."

"It is a message from Summer Day," said the warrior, further.

This made the trapper snatch up his line.

"I'll go with you, Messenger," said he.

159

And he hurried up the slope with them, envying the long and smooth elasticity of their steps.

They came to the chief, and found him like an angry statue in front of his lodge.

"Summer Day," said he, "returns word to me that the Iron Hand has dreamed, and that he deserves not that a warrior should fight him to prove that he is wrong, but that he should be whipped like a child until he realizes that he speaks the thing which is not true. He says that the Iron Hand is a boy, who has done nothing, taken no scalps, counted no coups, killed no enemies. Why should he be answered by a warrior and a wise man?"

# 32

They walked back through the camp together, Lessing and the boy. People looked at them with round eyes, for the tidings of the message had run like quicksilver through the camp.

"What will you do now, son?" asked Lessing.

"What I've known all along that I should have to do. I'll go to Summer Day's camp and find him, and fight him man to man."

"Why, Messenger, you're gone crazy. He'd have you clubbed to death by his young braves that are always wild to be the first to do what their medicine man wants!"

"Nevertheless," said the boy, "there is nothing else left for me to do. And I must be quick—I must be quick!'

He stopped short, stung by some idea, and then went on again, slowly, stepping softly as though he feared to break in upon his own ideas.

He did not see the girl coming toward them, carrying water to the lodge of her adopted father, but the trapper saw her, and the flash of her braided hair. And Lessing saw her falter, almost stop, and then come on with her eyes strictly lowered to the ground.

She was hurrying, and it seemed to the trapper that she had a shudder of satisfaction as she reached the lodge of her father.

Young Messenger saw her at the same time, and Lessing heard the intake of his breath.

Fixed in mid-stride, the boy paused there, with his face flushed, and his eye bright; and at the entrance flap the girl turned, as Lessing, somehow, knew that she must do. She turned, and her eyes widened with something more than surprise as she looked back to Messenger. More clearly than words or deeds, something happened between them in that instant before she stooped and passed quickly into the tepee.

Then Messenger went on his way, saying nothing, but his head was still high and his eyes were still brilliant.

In that moment, Lessing decided that he would make more than a short stay among the Blackfeet, for he saw that he might be needed by this youngster to keep him from taking some irremediable step.

The thought haunted him all that day. In the evening, Bray came back walking on air. He found that he had been accepted everywhere in the village with a perfect courtesy. Warriors had stopped and talked with him. Children had smiled at him.

"It's Messenger!" said Bray. "They all ask me questions about him. I ain't got enough Blackfoot lingo to answer; I ain't got enough information, neither. But I was popular everywhere, because they all wanted to talk about how he killed the deer at six hundred yards, and how he shot the head off the squirrel—and I guess you've heard the rest of the stories?"

"I've got something else to think about," said Lessing honestly.

And he had. It kept him awake that evening in his bed in the lodge of War Lance, and it was late before he closed his eyes. There was trouble ahead, as he saw it, for young Messenger, and if he escaped from the wiles of the medicine man, there were other dangers that he might worry about.

At last Lessing slept, but it seemed to him that he had hardly closed his eyes, when a whisper ran through the camp, like a gust of wind, and then the clang of a rifle shot jerked him to his feet.

A hundred voices were shouting one thing: "The Crows! The Crows!"

That babble was overcome by the roar of a lion's voice. It was War Lance, shouting his orders, even while he flung the saddle on the back of his favorite horse. Like eight arrows whirring to the mark, came the eight of his bodyguard for their mounts. They snatched their bridles from the hands of the squaw of War Lance. Almost instantly they were mounted.

Both the trapper and young Messenger were much behind them, and it seemed that every available man in the village already had flowed out to the south, where the attack was being delivered.

The squaws and children were out, as a matter of course; but they made way for the riders, and screeched encouragement as the white men went past, with Bray thundering at their heels, the last of all.

Out they galloped past the fringe of the lodges, only to find that the need for them already had vanished.

The Crows, attacking in much force, had nevertheless expected easier going than they found, and the sentinel system of War Lance had detected them while they still were at a little distance. A flurry of rifle shots had checked and turned them, and now they were retreating to wait for a better day.

All up the valley through which the little stream flowed, the whoops and the screeches of the fighters echoed and rang. And the explosions of the rifles showed like the flare of great fireflies. As the Blackfeet skirmished forward into the ravine, the Crows were retreating, not rapidly, but slowly, as people unwilling to press a fight in which they gained no advantage. Victories in Indian warfare are not counted glorious so much because of the number of the enemy slain as because of the impunity with which the damage is inflicted.

Every step of their retreat made the Crows stronger, because the walls of the ravine drew together like a funnel and gathered them in a more solid line.

The trapper and Bray, looking on, rode on more slowly toward the fight, leaving the screaming voices of the village behind them, advancing closer to the shouting warriors. Once fairly committed to the ravine, they found that the roar of the guns and the human voices was deafening. The Blackfeet were coming to a standstill, or advancing very slowly, feeling their way among the brush and the boulders.

"Where's Messenger?" shouted Bray suddenly, in the ear of the trapper.

Lessing looked back.

There was no sign of Messenger!

Either some accident to his horse, or the loosening of a girth, had caused him to fall back, or else—

Might it not be that the story of Summer Day was the perfect truth, and that fearless as young Messenger was in hand-to-hand fighting, he did not care for the sound of guns?

He shook his head, but the thought would not leave him; then, with a shrug of his strong shoulders, he went on with Bray to join the fighting Indians.

# 33

But Messenger, as he galloped out with his two white companions toward the fight, had had a new idea the instant that he saw the battlefield, and when the thought struck him, he drew in his horse to a stand.

Yonder, the valley drew together to a point. There was merely, at the head of it, a narrow bridle path that wound along close to the cliff, between the water and the mountain. On the other side of the stream sheer rock went straight up from the border of the swiftly flowing water.

Now, as his idea came to him, it made his heart leap with joy. For the ravine was a bottle. The Blackfeet closed the bottom of it solidly. The ravine walls were unclimbable and there was only the narrow mouth of the valley that needed corking.

He wondered that such a chief as War Lance had not seen the thing. Perhaps he would, later on. In the first place, he simply had galloped out to be in the midst of his men as they attacked the enemy.

Loudly the boy now shouted for Lessing and Bray, but the two had swept forward, well out of hearing. He could not venture on in starlight to find them. Besides, whatever was done must be done quickly, for in a few minutes, no doubt, the rearward of the retreating Crows would be through the narrow gap and spreading out over the safer tableland behind it. Perhaps, from that point, they might swing about and attempt to deliver another attack upon the unguarded side of the town.

At any rate, he determined on acting alone, since it must be so. And he pulled his horse to the side, and started on a dead run for the hills.

Two or three women spotted him at once; and instantly their throats were straining on his name, hurling insults. He went on, heedless of their opinion.

The next moment, the pony was galloping up the slope, and he had enough work and thought to keep himself in the saddle safely. For the noise and the touch of the spurs had driven the pony half frantic with excitement. It galloped furiously, blindly, forward, carrying the rider up and up almost like a bird among the dark heights.

Over the first rise, he turned the pony to the left, and shot down a dizzy bank, thirty yards long, to the bottom of a depression. At the foot of it, the pony turned a complete somersault, and, taken unawares, young Messenger was hurled a rod ahead.

The wind was knocked out of his body. But when he regained his feet he found that the horse was gone. With it was gone his chance of quick retreat, in case he got to the vital spot and found the Crows already there.

He hesitated only for an instant. The roaring of the battle just beyond the shallow range of the hills called him more than the roar of the sea ever called a sailor. He ran on. There was, at least, not far to go, now. He came to a last upward pitch; beyond it the ground sloped down almost precipitously sharp, and there beneath him was the neck of the valley.

To his right extended the table-land, with the little creek flowing in a meandering line across it. To the left, the battle was rolling and thundering up the pass, crowding closer and closer to the exit.

But still the rearmost warriors were not there!

He took a breath, freshening his grip on the rifle, and began the descent. Halfway down, he lost both foot and hand hold. The rifle flew down before him and landed with a clang in the rocky, narrow floor of the trail. He himself followed after and well-nigh broke a shoulder as he struck.

But he was up at once. He dared not rub bruises or wait for a staggered brain to clear.

The rifle was the first care. He pressed his hands swiftly over it, and told himself that all was well with the mechanism. Then, staring down the pass, he made out, distinctly, the dark loom of a mounted man, coming toward him.

They were there—they were ready to pour over him and blot him out. On foot as he was, he had no retreat. There was enough power of man and beast, there, to dash him to atoms, unless he held the pass!

A boulder, a ponderous mass, lay at the verge of the trail, and getting his hand under the back rim of it, he managed to give it one half turn. He would have been glad to budge it a little further, but he only had succeeded in toppling it, because it lay in a state of balance.

However, it almost entirely blocked the path, now, and it afforded to him a perfectly safe breastwork.

Behind it he knelt down, and leveled his rifle over the top of it when the oncoming Indian was a scant ten yards away. To the boy, the starlight was as clear as the sun, now that he was looking down the familiar, faintly gleaming barrel of the rifle, with the stock tucked comfortably against his shoulder. All except his head was shielded by the rock.

And a sudden compunction came over him as he saw the

loftily nodding feather crest of the man before him. It was some notable warrior, some chief, perhaps, a man who had done great things among his people.

Should he lie there in safety and clip away the life of this brave as securely as a woman clips a flower in her garden?

He hesitated, panting with doubt, as he had done on that other day when he had faced the medicine man in the wood.

Then he set his teeth.

This was no fair, open-daylight fighter. He and his lot would gladly have rushed into the Blackfoot camp and slaughtered all whom they found there, old and young. So setting his teeth, he shouted a ringing warning, and pulled the trigger.

The hammer fell with a click, and a little jangling sound of broken metal. There the weapon had broken—at the very point of the lock! There was still the revolver. It jumped into his hand like a living thing.

The Indian had answered that warning shout with a frantic yell of fear, surprise, rage. But he seemed to know the meaning of that tell-tale click. And now he spurred his charger forward, still whooping at the top of his lungs.

There was no time for a careful bead.

It was plainly the plan of the red man to vault his horse over the boulder and spear the enemy as he flew across. So young Messenger pressed his back as close as he could against the stone wall and fired across his body.

The feathered brave swayed from his saddle and pitched down, the pony vaulted the rock and fled on up the table-land, whinneying. Straight behind him came another, and another.

The first man, Messenger stopped with a bullet through the head of the horse. The rider, plunging down, was stunned by the fall. The third of the procession, seeing what had happened to his two predecessors, wheeled his horse about and fled. He would have made an easy target, but Messenger was not there to slaughter. He was there to stop the mouth of the pass.

The fugitive, in the meantime, had fled back, yelling the alarm at the top of his lungs, and the retreat of the rear-most ranks was patently stopped.

They would rally again, of course. There was plenty of courage among the Crows. But in the meantime, Messenger felt that he could rely upon a short interval.

Red men love to talk before they act. There might be a short moment during which they would hold council. And that he could use to fortify his position.

To the feathered brave, the youth went first and by a leg dragged him from the water. He was rewarded by a feeble groan, and Messenger gritted his teeth. Dead men were better company for him, just then, than living prisoners, even if in bonds.

But he drew the wounded man from the stream, and tied his hands and lashed him with the bridle reins of the dead horse back to back with the stunned warrior who had fallen face down. He, too, was living.

But most valuable of all was a repeating Winchester rifle which the second brave had dropped in his fall.

Nine shots had been fired from it. From the pouch of the warrior himself, Messenger reloaded the gun and stood on guard.

The turmoil at the neck of the canyon had not been overlooked by the Blackfeet, it appeared. For now a great screeching and whooping arose from the farther end of the valley.

The Crows, between two millstones, were silent as a tomb.

Not for long. Perfectly well Messenger comprehended that the silence came before a storm, and that the storm would break in his direction. But, at the best, they would only be able to attack him two abreast—and in his hands was apparently an excellent rifle.

He tried it, half hating to waste the bullet, and heard the shot click against the rocks far down the ravine.

It was as though he had fired a signal shot.

Suddenly, out of the very ground before him, as it seemed, men arose and leaped in at him. He was lying behind the horse, now, a shallower and less perfect breast-work, but it gave him some protection, and a perfect rest for the rifle, as he lay flat.

Right into the faces of the oncoming braves he drove his bullets.

He upon the right of the foremost two swerved far out, and falling into the rapid waters of the stream was tumbled down the bed by it. He upon the left bounded into the air with a death-yell that ceased half uttered, as though a hand had been clapped over the agonized lips. Two more were behind. One of these stumbled forward upon his face. Then the rifle jammed as Messenger curled his finger to take the life of the fourth of that attack.

He dropped the useless weapon. With the revolver—he could bless now the hours of practice in making a swift and perfect draw—he shot upward, and the brave, staggering, turned and went uncertainly back down the trail, trying to run, but with his feet dragging.

Yonder in the back of the pass, Messenger could see only very indistinctly, but enough to make out that there was a general movement in retrogression, and he heard wailing voices of lament, groans of despair.

Back they rolled.

The pass was empty, just before him, and suddenly the boy was aware, for the first time, that waspish sounds had been humming about his head, and that his left shoulder was stinging badly. He felt it, and found that his sleeve was soaking wet with blood. However, it appeared to be no more than a surface scratch, for his left arm was still perfectly at his command.

He turned to his prisoners, then.

The groaning of the feathered brave had ceased; he might be dead, by now.

So young Messenger kneeled beside him and placed a hand over the man's heart.

It was beating steadily. He tried him in the Blackfoot tongue.

"My friend," said the boy, "where did the bullet strike you? Are you badly hurt?"

He had aimed for the head, he remembered, in that first attack.

And the voice of the brave answered him with a perfect calm, and in the only Indian dialect with which Messenger was familiar: "The bullet struck my head but it must have glanced along the skull. It struck me like a club, but I thought that I fell into the water."

"I drew you out," said Messenger. "Are you hurt in any other place?"

"My left shoulder was broken by the fall. Otherwise, I am not hurt."

"If your shoulder is hurt, then the rein of the bridle is torturing you," said Messenger.

"That is nothing," answered the other.

"What is your name?" asked Messenger.

"It is known among my people," said the warrior. "The Blackfeet also know me, if they have memories. You will hear me sing it in the fire."

"Fire?" cried the boy.

"He is Red Feather," said the other captive. "The women will taste his death for a long time."

"They will come again," said Red Feather slowly. "They will not remain there below. They will come again surely.

They know that I am here. My sworn blood brothers, they will not keep their lives while I lie here."

"Four men have come, and four men are dead," said the boy. "I don't think they'll try the pass again."

He stared down into the darkness. Then, cautiously, he loosened the bridle strap and shifted it under the injured shoulder of the chief. The latter, in spite of his resolution, could not help uttering a faint groan of relief.

"There will be no fire for you, Red Feather," said the boy.

"It is the new warrior of War Lance. It is the white man," said the companion of the chief, interrupting again.

"The Iron Hand—" said the chief slowly. "The Iron Hand, and the gentle heart. If you take your knife, now, and drive it into my heart, the spirits of the Crows who have gone before me will praise you in the sky, brother."

"There will be no fire," repeated the boy. "Not unless they burn me, also. Lie quietly, and trust to me for your life, if the Blackfeet come to you. I must keep watch. I think your friends are coming, as you promised. Heaven help them."

# 34

Straining his sight into the dark of the hollow, Messenger thought, again and again, that he saw shadowy forms before him. But his eyes deceived him.

At the bottom of the ravine, the Blackfeet, still slowly

advancing, made the place ring with pandemonium; in between, the Crows were still as silent as death. And death, perhaps, already had come to some of them.

Messenger made sure that all was as well as could be, and returning to the Crows, he separated them, and bound them by their hands to jagged projections of the boulder which he had overturned in the trail. In this manner, they were able to sit up and look over the scene. The boy crouched beside them. He had taken up a third rifle, one that had fallen from the hand of the second warrior to die under his bullets.

"Why did you leave the pass unguarded, Red Feather," said he, "if you are the leader of this band?"

"Because I was a child," said Red Feather. "All the blood that has been spilled here, it flows out of my folly. All the scalps that are taken are torn from my head. All the shame of the Crows is my shame. But I was a child. It was hard to hold back my men. They were hungry to rush through the village, and every one of my young men already saw the red scalp of War Lance hanging at his bridle. So we charged, and were turned. But when we had to retreat, then I looked up the pass and recognized the trap. I hurried on with Straight Arrow, who sits here beside me in sorrow, and two others, to get to the trap and hold it. But it closed on me. It set its teeth in me, and here I sit and wait for the end."

Still they looked together down the valley, when a sound of shouting beat up to them, and there was a roar of many hoofs of horses, galloping together.

"They charge! They charge!" shouted Straight Arrow.

"Go home, good lance!" yelled Red Feather. "Knife, find the heart and the throat! Bullets, drive true! Axes strike, and clubs shatter skulls! Kill the Blackfeet dogs! Count coups, rip away scalps! Take glory, glory, back to the Crows!"

As he shouted this war cry in a vast, whooping voice, and ended with a yell that fairly curdled the blood of Messenger, the firing in the valley redoubled.

Then the almost straight line of the fireflies, whose gleaming had marked the position of the Blackfeet, grew irregular. In some places it swayed forward. In others, it sagged back.

"Kill, kill!" shrieked Straight Arrow. "Now for honor! Now for the scalp dance! Oh, my brothers, strike hard."

And he and the chief, Red Feather, whooped frightfully in unison.

The flashing of the guns in the valley formed a great, irregular pattern, out of which appeared a long, streaming point of those deadly, gleaming fireflies, and behind them glowed a more thickly clustered group.

"The Crows have not driven the Blackfeet before them!" cried out Red Feather, suddenly. "They have only broken through, and now they flee for their lives, and the Blackfeet follow on their swift horses, striking down the laggards, spearing them, counting many coups. Do you hear their battle yell rising, Straight Arrow? It is the Blackfeet, the howling of dogs!"

The fighting scattered far and wide across the increasing width of the plain, and the voices of the triumphant Blackfeet flowed back toward the site of the victory.

Out of that hollow, now, there went up, here and there, wild whoopings and yells of victory. And, amidst other sounds, a mournful chanting.

"Listen, listen!" said Red Feather. "It is a Blackfoot. One of the dogs now is howling his death song!"

"It is good," said Straight Arrow, in a voice of infinite satisfaction.

"Oh, Crows," said the chief, in a voice of desire, "have you struck your wings in their faces, and your claws in their hearts? What scalps have you taken? What coups have you counted? No, no," he added gloomily. "You were fleeing. You were fighting for your lives. Your chief put you in a trap, and the trap has closed, and the women of our nation will curse the day that Red Feather led the warriors out to the battle!"

"They will trade you back to your people," said the boy suddenly, "for something that they wish—for a long peace, perhaps, or for horses. Well, you will live to see men following you on the warpath again, Red Feather."

And Straight Arrow suddenly struck in: "It is true that no Blackfoot closed the pass behind you."

"True," said the chief, pondering the thought. "Who could have known that with War Lance there was a man of such a medicine as this? Their phophet was not with them, Summer Day was not there. But the Iron Hand was there—he looked through the dark. His eye, like the eye of a night-flying owl, flew through the night and saw the place where he should stand. He went there with his iron hand. With it he closed the pass. It is true, Straight Arrow, that a great medicine was against me in this fight. Will the Crows remember?"

"The Crows will remember, in time," suggested Straight Arrow. "They will remember all the better after other enemies of the Blackfeet have learned to know the Iron Hand. The Assiniboines, and the Cheyennes, and the Pawnees will feel his hand."

The hoofs of horses rang now, up the trail that led toward the pass, and a voice shouted loudly toward them, in the Blackfoot tongue. The boy did not answer, at once, and the voice called again: "Who are here? What heroes of the Blackfeet are here who closed the pass?"

"I am here," said the voice of Messenger in answer.

His intonation of the tongue, slightly untrue, seemed familiar to them. A sudden shout answered him.

"It is the Iron Hand! He has closed the pass."

The hoofbeats came closer.

"Stop!" called Messenger. "What chief is there?"

"Strong Bow is here. Strong Bow, come closer and speak to him. He is stopping us for some reason."

"I am here," called a deep, rather husky voice. "What is it that you wish, brother?"

"There are with me," said the boy, "two brave Crows."

"Dead men?" broke out the impatient voice of the chief.

"One dead man fell in the stream and was carried down among the rocks. Two dead men lie in the path before you. Be careful with your horses. Two living men are here with me."

"Living men!" shouted many voices.

And the boy, who was close to Red Feather, felt the shudder of his muscular body.

"Let us have them! Let us have the prisoners!"

"They are his own until the scalp dance!" answered the commanding voice of the chief. "Iron Hand, you have done great deeds. Come with your prisoners, or we will put them on our horses, if they cannot walk."

"Wait where you are!" commanded Messenger. "These are my prisoners. I want them to be safely kept."

"They must die!" answered the chief instantly.

"They must live," replied Messenger firmly, "and they must be traded back to their people for whatever you wish—horses or other captives!"

"Brother," said Strong Bow, "you are like one who puts food into the mouths of the starving, and then snatches it away again. Have they names, the two men with you, or are they young braves, fighting their first fight?"

"Whatever their names may be," replied the boy, "I make this bargain with you, Strong Bow. They must live. I must have your word, or else send for War Lance, and he will give his word instead."

Very audibly, he heard the groan of the chief.

"What other men are with you, Iron Hand?" said he. "If you led them to that place and fought as their leader, the chief glory is yours; but they have a right to lift their voices and say what shall be done with the prisoners they have helped to capture."

"Yes!" shouted the other Blackfeet. "They have their right. They have their battle right. Let us hear their voices. What other brave men have been counting coups with you, Iron Hand?"

A slight tingling passed up the back of Messenger. He took a breath, and then he answered quietly, for he was swelling with instinctive pride. "There are no others. There is only one voice to speak about these men, my friends!"

Strong Bow started to reply, when a yell of wonder stopped him.

It was a moment or so before Strong Bow could make himself heard, and then he cried out: "If you have such a strong medicine that you alone could stand in front of all the warriors and turn them back like sheep before a wolf— if you alone could do that, brother, the men are yours. Do with them what you will. No Blackfoot will touch them. But the old women will gnash their teeth when they see the murdering Crows in safety."

"Now," said the boy, "I give you their names. You have given me your word in exchange, Strong Bow?"

"I have given my word," said the chief. "Now, tell us their names?"

"First, there is a warrior and a strong man called Straight Arrow."

There was a veritable groan from among the Blackfeet.

"We know him!" they said in unison, and a single voice added: "I have a token of him in my side. Why do I ride bent over, except because of Straight Arrow? Must he be left free and safe?"

"I have given my word," said Strong Bow. "I must protect him like a brother, though I had rather be handling his heart. What is the other name, Iron Hand?"

"A name you know, Strong Bow. The other is a great chief, and his name is Red Feather!"

The youth stepped back as he spoke, like one braced against a strong wind, and he had reason, for the screech of rage that rose from those warriors was enough to drive needlepoints of apprehension through his brain.

"We are dead men," said Red Feather. "Let us stand up, Iron Hand, and die on our feet, like warriors and men!"

"Strong Bow!" shouted the boy. "I have your promise! The honor of a chief is pledged to me. Red Feather is now like a blood brother to you, while he is in our party!"

Strong Bow himself pushed to the front.

His shout forced the others to be obediently silent, though their silence was rather a deep growling in their throats.

"It is true," said he. "I have given my word. It is stronger than my hand to break my promise. Now give them to us freely, and each of them is as safe as though he were my father's son!"

# 35

It was, on the whole, very sad business for the Crows. They had left many and many a one of their best warriors dead on the bottom of that ravine. They streamed away through a close rifle fire which could not help but tell on them, no matter how hard they flogged their ponies, or how they lay along the sides of the horses.

Lessing and Bray had done their business for the Blackfeet in the coolest and most logical manner. When they saw what was likely to happen, they simply had dismounted and taken a good position on a slight, rough rise of ground. Each of them faced toward opposite sides, and when the charge of the Crows came, their horsemen naturally split around that slight eminence, like water flowing around a boat. Bray and Lessing, lying in perfect comfort and safety, emptied their rifles at close range.

As the Blackfeet went off like a cloud of hornets behind their foes, the trapper and his companion sat up and stared up the valley.

"That War Lance," said the younger man, "he's got a brain. I never would've thought of corkin' up that ravine, that way."

"That War Lance is a wise man," admitted the trapper, "but that ain't any reason that we should overlook some of the things that are laid out right here at our feet!"

So they went down, of one mind, to plunder fallen horse and fallen man. There was plenty that was worth taking. Lessing got a steel battle-ax with a richly decorated handle; two excellent Indian saddles, no fewer than four knives, a beaded suit in perfectly good condition, a good, new, repeating rifle, and over twenty pounds of ammunition.

His horse had run away during the charge, while its master was lying prone among the rocks, but Lessing more than recouped himself by catching two wandering ponies which he found riderless in the ravine. On these he carefully loaded his spoils; Bray had been similarly occupied and had gained even greater spoils.

He had gained something more than spoils. He had won peace of mind, for it was not likely that the Blackfeet would foolishly hold old grudges against a man who had just showed his feeling by fighting for them.

In the meantime, the warriors returned from the pursuit. They had cut down those who were mounted on slow horses, or those who lagged because of wounds. They came back like ravens to the battlefield, and into the ravine, also, the women came with torches, shrieking in their exultation as they found the plunder of the fallen.

A rumor swept the ravine. A single man had dared to go to the head of the valley and close it against the retreat of the Crows.

Old Lessing shook his head.

"There's the start and the makin's of a grand lie," suggested Lessing. "If any one man did do such a job, he's gunna be more famous than War Lance himself, and all in one stroke. But no one man would ever've dared to try such a thing."

"No," agreed Bray. "Nobody in the world. Besides, I seen the winkin' of the rifle fire, and it must've been three or four men up there, shootin' side by side. We'll get the truth, pretty quick! We'll find out what it's all about. But where's your friend Messenger, that you thought so much of?"

"Aw, he'll turn up," answered the trapper, embarrassed.

"Yeah," replied the other. "It'll be about the right time for him to turn up, maybe—after the shootin' is over!"

Lessing, for some reason, found no word to say against this, at the time being. He started with Bray across the ravine, leading their captured war ponies. They had headed back for the encampment, by this time, but they checked themselves to watch a procession which was coming down the side of the ravine. It was made bright by the burning of several torches, which the first women from the town were carrying. They whirled the torches and screeched with their joy.

Other sounds of a different nature were ringing through the ravine, the isolated whoops of the rejoicing warriors, the laughter of the women; and, here and there, a sudden outburst of lamenting as one of the torch carriers who hunted among the fallen came upon a husband or a relative lying dead.

But Bray and old Lessing paid no heed to anything except the procession.

"They're bringing down the heroes that stopped up the end of the ravine, and heroes they are," said Lessing. "I'd like to see their ugly faces myself, Bray. Let's get over there and watch 'em go by."

So they pressed to the side of the ravine in time to see, first of all, the bodyguard of the great War Lance coming down the slope. They were intact, but they showed that they had been through the hottest kind of water. No lances were carried. These must have been broken in hand-to-hand fighting. A bullet had ripped open the face of one of the youngest of these distinguished braves, but he rode on, and carelessly allowed the blood to dry and blacken.

Others had been struck, as the dark patches on their clothing showed, but none was incapacitated, and they looked wilder and more formidable, now, than they had when riding into the gate of Fort Lippewan. Behind them came the chief himself. He had headed the pursuit of the enemy, and then rapidly returning, he had gone up the valley after Strong Bow to find the heroes.

Just to the rear of the great war chief himself came Strong Bow.

He was on foot, and he led a horse in each hand. Upon one was mounted a badly wounded Crow; upon the other sat a Crow whose face was a mass of ugly wounds, but who sat straight enough.

"That's Red Feather, or I miss my guess," said Lessing. "If they've got him, they've got the Crows in their pockets, I tell you."

As they came nearer, the flaring, shaken light of their torches shone brilliantly upon the object of their admiration, and Bray grasped the shoulder of his companion.

"By glory," he breathed, "it's that boy—it's that Messenger!"

It was Messenger, in fact.

He was mounted on a pony not selected at hazard from the spoils, but given by the hands of War Lance himself. And, at the first glance, it was seen that the war chief of the Blackfeet had bestowed his own best charger upon the white man. A steel-dust gray, glancing and brilliant with sweat, it fairly danced down the ravine, with young Messenger sitting almost gloomily in the saddle. That compliment was not foolishly paid by War Lance. It was like a crown on the head of Messenger, however. And at the sight of the horse and the man, realizing what the thing meant, the squaws went half insane with joy. They whooped, and screamed, and lifted their strong hands toward the boy.

"That's him, and there's only one of him," said Lessing,

with an infinite satisfaction. "Look at him, boy, and look at him ag'in! He stopped up the ravine like a cork in the bottle. He's gone and got himself more famous in one evening's work, than most big chiefs do in a whole life."

"It's him," said Bray hoarsely. "Let's get on to the camp. There's gunna be a lot of feastin' and whoopin' and dancin', tonight!"

They turned together, and made rapidly toward the camp.

# 36

Just as the dogs of a village clamor and clatter with their barking, and two or three big timber wolves come down to the edges of the cultivated fields to howl a dismal answer, so the people of the Blackfoot village clattered and whooped, and shouted in their joy; but, here and there, a few voices went up to the sky more dolefully than the crying of wolves. There were the women lamenting for their dead.

There were few killed. Plenty of wounds, from slight to serious, had been distributed through the tribe; but for that great victory, they had paid with only three lives, all lost when the Crow charge broke through the defending line of the Blackfeet. Three lives were a very slight payment for such an overwhelming triumph; but the mourners must be heard.

The mourners paused to let the triumphal procession

pass by, and when it did so, the sound of the wailing became dim in the rear. Yet it never passed entirely out of the mind of Messenger. It hung there like a dark cloud.

The rather deliberate and slow approach of the procession of victory had been preceded by a rush of most of the women and warriors into the village, and there the preparations for the scalp dance were made at once. It was rare for a tribe to have such a chance of rejoicing. Usually, their warriors came back lean and dusty from the warpath, and the hint of what they had done had long come in before them, but this was another matter. Here the smell of the smoke of battle was fresh in all nostrils. And with eager hands they set about building the great pile for the fire.

They had freshened their paint for the festival. Their faces were hideous with deliberate intent. If they had seemed terrible to the enemy, their purpose was now to exemplify the terror which they had caused. Several of them, however, who were favored with surface wounds which were not dangerous, disdained paint and allowed the dried or still oozing blood to speak by itself, and, on the whole, they were the most hideous of the lot. A number carried fresh scalps, some of them clotted with gore, and the sight was almost too horrible for Messenger to watch. For he could not help feeling that practically every death which had occurred among the Crows was due to his action in blocking the pass.

Moreover, he detested this publicity and would gladly have left the scene, but he could not do so with any grace. For the attentions of the bodyguard of War Lance had been, by his order, transferred to the white lad, and they were grouped closely around him. He could not stir unattended by them. When he rose from the place where he had been asked to take his seat on the ground near the fire, the eight rose in turn, and looked at him with expectant faces. And he was forced to take his seat again.

All around the fire they were gathered in a great circle, those fighters of the Blackfeet, and behind them stood the youths on the verge of manhood, those almost ready to pass the final test of torture before being acclaimed as brave. Yet behind these, and mingled among them, were the women and smaller children, and some of the squaws held up little infants, with shining faces, in order to look on at the wild ceremony.

The fire, in the meantime, had mounted to the top of the pyre and threw vast red and golden arms into the sky.

So great was the heat that the face of Messenger almost blistered, but the Indians seemed untroubled by it. Drums began to beat in furious cadences. Every now and then, memory of the battle forced some brave to spring to his feet with an echoing war cry, and twenty men would leap up and rival him at once.

Now the great war chief strode out before his people. Utter silence fell all around him.

He was seen to fill his pipe, holding it in a peculiar fashion, with the bowl to one side, and the stem pointing downward at a slant to the left. After it had been filled, he took from the verge of the fire a living coal that sparkled like a jewel with its power, and transferred it with a lightning dexterity to the surface of the tobacco in the pipe bowl. A few whiffs started the pipe, and then he blew smoke to the deities of the upper air, to the underground spirits, and north, east, south and west, very solemnly.

These proceedings were watched with awe and in deepest silence. Afterward, he said: "Oh, my people, today we have had good fortune. The Sky People have been kind to us. And now is the time for us to count our coups and show the scalps which we have taken, according to the custom of our fathers. Let every man tell the truth. Let every man search his heart before he speaks. First of all, there is one who must talk to us and tell us what he did. He must tell us what spirits inspired him, and how they helped him to fight. Otherwise, what man could have done what he has done? His medicine is very strong. That I knew when I first saw him, and I was happy when he came riding with me to visit my people. He is going to stay a year among us—"

Here, in spite of their respect for their chief, a wild whoop of jubilance rose from a hundred throats. It died out slowly, and when he could be heard again, War Lance continued: "If we can prove to him that we are his brothers, perhaps he will become one of us, always—"

Another loud yell of approval went up at this.

Said War Lance: "We wait for you, brother. Let the Iron Hand stand up and tell us how he acted, when the Crows came down like wolves and hoped to eat us like so many sheep."

He paused, there was a stir, a whisper, and then a murmur of disappointment.

Two or three of the bodyguard leaned close to the boy and tried to persuade him, but what was ceremonial to the Blackfeet was boasting to him.

The pause grew and grew.

Suddenly an old warrior uttered a shout, and rising from the ground, threw off his robe and stood in the flushing light of the fire. He must have been at least sixty years old, but only his long, straggling hair had turned white. His legs and arms were burnished with long, hard strips of muscle, undisguised by an ounce of fat.

Old though he was, he was as erect as a youth, and every eye noted instantly that a scalp dangled from the truncheon of his spear. It was plain that he had been in the thick of the fight. Now that his robe was thrown off, he appeared flashing with paint—bright streaks of red, yellow, green, and blue, covered his body and his face, and contrasted with the silvery shower of his long hair which became, when he moved violently, like a mist blowing about his shoulders.

185

"It is Striking Eagle," whispered one of the bodyguard to Messenger, "and the spirits have most surely spoken to him."

He appeared, at least, like one who sees a light dimly, and follows it with an outstretched hand. So, like a sleep-walker, his head thrown far back, he advanced toward the fire.

There he paused, holding the same attitude. The eyes of the Blackfeet, all around Messenger, were fairly bulging with awe. And, looking across the circle of the firelight, he saw the face of Yellow Antelope, transformed with excitement, her hands clasped as she prepared to hear miracles.

"I have seen it!" said the old brave. "The spirits show me the truth. The eye of a hawk is in me, looking out and seeing all the things which the Iron Hand did tonight."

War Lance, without a word, stepped back to the edge of the circle and waited with folded arms.

"First," said the warrior, "I see him roused from the lodge of the great chief. The others leap out. But the Iron Hand goes more slowly. Where there is strength, there is also patience. He goes more slowly. Their galloping horses leave him. He comes out upon the valley where the fighting is. You have seen the valley. O Blackfeet!"

There was a brief shout of agreement from the warriors.

"The Iron Hand looks over the battle. He sees that the Crows retreat. He sees the narrow head of the valley. He holds up his hands to the Sky People. He calls out to them and he says: 'My fathers, shall I call upon the warriors of the Blackfeet to go with me to stop the Crows?'

"So he calls out to them, and the Sky People, who love him, come down close above his head, so that he can hear the swishing of their bodies in the air, and they answer him: 'There is no time to call for others, and your own strength is sufficient!'

"When he hears this, he doubts no more, neither does

he linger. Who of you has seen the hare fleeing? Who has seen the antelope racing over the plains? Who has seen the forest fire jumping from mountain to mountain in a great wind? That is how the Iron Hand rushed toward the danger. He did not turn his back. He had no fear. He laughed as he went, and the Sky People flying above him laughed also and exulted in the warrior. His horse fell and then ran away, with its reins flying in the wind, but the Iron Hand laughed, and went on. He was swifter than the wind. He came to the high place above the pass. You know the place, O Blackfeet!"

There was the same deep-throated, rumbling response as before.

"He looked down. He could see the fighting in the ravine, and he could hear the guns and the shouting. Below him the pass was dark, like the throat of a well. It was a great distance. We all have seen the cliff. But the Iron Hand was not afraid. He laughed, and leaped out into the thin, dark air. Behold! It received him with hands. It lowered him gently to the trail below.

"Then he saw beside the trail a great rock. Eight strong men could hardly lift it—"

There was an involuntary shout of testimony on this point, and a murmur of admiration following it.

Striking Eagle went on with his speech, but it became less speech than pantomime. He began to dance and bound about the fire, illustrating his "inspired" picture of how the Iron Hand had met the enemy and thrust them back. He counted coups, he made shouting speeches of defiance, and when he had ended, he was so exhausted that he was barely able to retire to a place in the circle of watchers.

His place was taken by another, a formidable warrior of mature years, with a face like a weather-scarred rock. He told how in the charge of the Crows for freedom two braves had borne down upon him just as he fired his last bullet, and how he flung his shield edgewise at one of them, and dodged the battle-ax of the second, then stabbed him in the side with a knife as the victim went past him.

He was followed by another and by another.

The enthusiasm of the warriors could not now be restrained. Half a dozen of the braves would be in the circle at the same time, shouting, dancing, yelping out their own praises.

Young Messenger, watching the crowd, began to see and hear them no longer as individuals, but rather as units lost in one great picture. An absurd or a hideous picture it might have seemed to men dwelling securely in Eastern cities, but out there between the mountains, and under the stars, it was a different matter. Nothing had happened in his life like this. Certainly nothing had given him such a thrilling sense of pride and power.

# 37

There were two days of noisy feasting for the tribe, after this glorious victory, for such it appeared to them. Bob Messenger spent his time very largely by himself, and, as Bray said to old Lessing, the boy seemed to be moving in a dream.

"He oughta be in a dream," said Lessing. "He's been offered about a hundred hosses, guns, new lodges, everything that a man could want to set up in Injun life. He oughta be in a dream."

"He's thinking about old Summer Day," answered Bray.

"Maybe he is, and maybe not," said the trapper. "Likely we ain't gunna hear from Summer Day."

It was the main subject of conversation throughout the camp. The great medicine man had declined the first challenge on what appeared to the tribesmen sufficient grounds. He was a chief of established power, and the young white lad had accomplished nothing in war. This was now all changed. Whether he wanted them or not, at least five coups were attributed to young Messenger, and five coups won in a single fight were tenfold more glorious than if they had been picked up in the course of a long career. They were, moreover, "first coups," all of them.

And that very night of the battle, without delaying, War Lance had dispatched one of the lightest of his young men with three horses and orders to ride like mad to the camp of the medicine man and return in haste with the answer of Summer Day. For that answer the braves were now waiting. And Messenger waited with them.

But, as had been suggested, there was something more than the medicine man in the mind of the boy. He had not passed into a dream, as Bray thought. In fact, it seemed to him that he was stepping out of a dream into reality. And one of those realities was as poignant as the odor of spring flowers.

He lounged, one morning, in the lodge of War Lance, who had just reached a momentous decision. His hatred of the Crows was as strong as that of any of his men, but in the presence of the two great warriors as captives, he saw a means to a great end. If they were sent home without ransom, without exchange asked, to their tribe, safe and sound, the Crows, whose spirits must have been a little daunted by their late defeat, would hardly fail to come to terms of peace with such strong and magnanimous foemen. Therefore, he had decided to dismiss them, and even to send them with presents, as became a great war chief. With this decision, the village was buzzing, and War Lance himself was at a feast where he would explain his policy to the wise old men of the tribe. Bray and Lessing were off hunting, and there remained in the lodge only the white boy and the squaw of the chief.

He said to her, suddenly: "When young men wish to marry, what do they do among the Blackfeet?"

She bent her head a little lower over the quill work which engaged her.

"They take horses and tie them to the lodge entrance of the father of the girl they wish to have for a wife," she said.

"I have no horses," he said bluntly. "But I suppose I could buy them."

"You have a name," she answered. "Leave that at the door of the lodge. Go speak to the father, and if he is a wise man, he will take his daughter's hand and put it in yours."

"You are a kind woman," said the boy.

Suddenly he sighed. "I must not go like a beggar," he said.

"There is no chief among the Blackfeet and no rich man who would not give you twenty horses to buy a wife," she declared.

"There again, it is giving, giving, giving, and all on the part of your tribe. I have been here these days sitting and eating, and taking your good things, and giving nothing!"

"Except your blood for us!" she said softly.

He waved this suggestion away.

"But first a man must have the consent of the girl," he said.

"Yes. That is true. I remember when Crazy Elk offered thirty horses, even, for the hand of Green Willow, and her father took the horses, but afterward he had to give them back, because the girl laughed in the face of that man."

"Did she laugh at him?"

"Yes, and made him a fool before all the tribe."

"What should I do first?" asked the boy. "I see that the young men do not talk to the girls of the Blackfeet."

"In the early evening," said the squaw, "when the heat of the middle day is over, then the young women go down to the edge of the river to bring up water."

"Yes," said the boy, "I think that I've seen them go. What of that? Shall I go and offer to carry up the water for her?"

The squaw laughed.

"No woman would let a warrior carry a burden for her," she answered. "She would be shamed through her whole life, if she did such a thing. But if you watch, you will see that the girls do not go down when the young men swim, nor above, where the horses are driven to water, nor above that; but still at a greater distance there is an easy bank down to the edge of the stream, and the girls go there and get the water, where it runs pure.

"As they come back, sometimes here and there stands a brave with a blanket wrapped about him. When he sees the one he wishes to speak to, he steps to her quickly and throws the blanket about her so that it covers them both and no eye can see them. You must do the same thing. If she will stand still and listen to you, you may be happy. If she speaks and says 'No,' then there is no further hope for you. If she speaks and at once says 'Yes,' then you are sure to marry her, if you can find enough horses or enough fame to please the heart of her father. Go to the bank, therefore, wrapped in a blanket. Otherwise, the small boys will see you and know you and mock even the Iron Hand. Small boys fear nothing in the world, not even the strongest man!"

Messenger laughed, very faintly. His heart beat uneasily.

"Go down to the river, therefore," went on the squaw, "and when you see the shine of her yellow hair as she comes up to the top of the bank—"

He started. He found that she was smiling very broadly at him.

"What do you know?" he asked.

"Oh," said she, "I am very busy, but between times I look up from my work and see a little sunlight through the edges of the lodge entrance. Sometimes I even hear a little more than the whistle in the wind."

The youth sat very still.

"What will she say?" he burst out suddenly.

The squaw dropped her needle and made a gesture with both hands.

"When the blanket is around her, ask, and then you will be the first to know!"

That was late in the morning, but it seemed to Messenger that the day lasted a long year before the sun began to slide down the western arch of the sky, and he saw the girls of the village go out to draw the water.

At last he took from the lodge of War Lance a great buffalo robe, and felt the smile of the squaw following him as he walked toward the river.

He was nervous. Twice he actually stopped and was about to turn back, but he mastered himself, and went on. He rehearsed in his mind everything that the squaw had told him, but suddenly he was disturbed by a loud pealing of boyish laughter.

He turned, and there were a dozen bronzed urchins, rocking with mirth.

Mirth directed toward him! And why? They pointed. And they were designating his shoes and trousers which the robe did not cover. Of course, no other man in the tribe would be wearing such apparel as this!

And he ground his teeth, but drawing a great breath, he went on. At least, he would not wear a mask which was no mask at all. And, throwing the robe across his shoulder, like a useless cloak, he strode on his way.

The boys followed him, dancing. And one of them, the oldest of the lot, sang out in a voice like the crowing of a rooster: "May the golden color be real gold to you, O Iron Hand!"

# 38

The boys left him, scampering back toward the swimming pool, doubtless to spread the news. They were gone now, but the tingle of their mirth still disturbed him. Yet he went on.

He felt that he was doing a frightful thing. For how would the civilized women of the East treat this child of Nature? How would they sneer at her lack of social poise? Yet he could not leave her behind him. She fitted into all that he desired. There was the medicine man to be disposed of, but after that, she was the final consummation of life.

With the robe still hanging idly over his shoulder, Messenger reached, at last, the edge of the bank overlooking the stream. On the verge of the water he could see the Indian girls stooping to fill their vessels. Was Yellow Antelope there? Was she among those who leaned above the water and then stood there a moment, chattering so pleasantly?

A gleam beside him, along the path, made him turn. And there she was! She was going down toward the water, but when she saw his face, she started aside as a deer might start when there is a strange noise in the brush, and her eyes widened as she looked at him.

It was not joy that opened them, he could tell himself. It was not the same look which he had felt upon him as she looked across the fire toward him, during the scalp dance. But there was recognition and knowledge in it.

Did she know, also, for what woman he had come? How was it that the entire camp understood so well?

He grew angry, as he grew mystified, and his face was stern as he stood there, watching the girls coming up the path, but they halted, far away, as though they saw Yellow Antelope approaching the Iron Hand, and wished to observe what happened.

He stepped forward, flinging the robe around her. They were covered completely by it.

He spoke, and the Blackfoot tongue made his voice deeper than usual, and graver.

"Yellow Antelope," he said, "I have come here to ask you to be my squaw, and live with me the rest of your life."

She opened her eyes wide, and looked at him.

It seemed to him that she was not troubled by his nearness, but that she was searching into his eyes, in the effort to find there some hidden secret.

Then she spoke, and the sound of her voice so moved him that at first he hardly understood her meaning, but at last he knew that she was saying, "No!" and three times over that she had repeated it.

"No!"

Why should he be so surprised? Why should he feel that the thing which he heard was unreal, and that it could not be that he had heard aright.

Then, stunned and terrified, as he found himself losing her, he cried out, loudly: "Is there some other man?"

She shook her head. Her hand pushed against his breast.

"Let me go!" said she.

And he stepped back, slowly, and the robe fell back over his arm, while the girl went on hurriedly, with a bowed, shining head.

The brightness seemed, at a stroke, to have been taken from the day.

And through the purple quiet of the evening he saw the other girls coming up the path. One after another they went past him, and they gave him no regard but stared straight ahead, as though they had seen some catastrophe.

# 39

Very slowly Messenger went on back to the camp. When he reached it, he made out that the news had gone there before him, and that it had an odd effect upon the Blackfeet. The little boys stared at him, but they no longer laughed. The young braves whom he passed kept their heads downcast and pretended not to see him go by.

It was amazing that they should have heard the news of his repulse so suddenly, and that they took it so seriously.

And then, going by the lodge in which Yellow Antelope lived, he heard a faint pulse of sobbing coming from within.

He knew that Indian etiquette forbade his entrance into that lodge, and, therefore, he went straight on to the tepee of War Lance. The squaw was still at her work, and when he entered, she lifted her head and gave him a long, fixed look.

"She said 'No' at once, and that was the end of it," said the boy.

The squaw nodded.

"She is young," said she. "She is very, very young, my friend. But a man who walks a long trail is sure to come to a turning, is he not?"

"What do you mean by that?" asked the boy curiously.

"Why should she say 'No'?" asked the woman.

"Because I don't please her, of course."

"Three things displease an Indian girl," said the squaw. "Cowardice, poverty, and a foolish brain. Are you a coward, or poor, or a fool?"

This simple enumeration made the boy blink.

"It's not as simple as that," he argued. "Besides, she's not an Indian. Her skin is as white as mine."

"What is the color of the skin? The color of the heart is what matters, Iron Hand, and she has lived almost all her life among the Blackfeet. What they are, she is!"

"You make riddles for me," said he. "I don't understand them at all."

"Do you want a wife to take with you, or a wife to leave here among her people?"

"Why, a wife to take with me," said the boy. "That, of course."

"And married in the white man's way, forever?"

"Yes, forever."

At this, the squaw shook her head decidedly.

"Then she is not such a fool. It makes an Indian sad to give up her country. If you like her here, you may not like her when she is in the house of the whites."

"How can that be?" he asked. "She will be herself, no matter where she is."

"She will not," answered the squaw firmly. "What would a prairie dog do in a forest, and what would a tree squirrel do in the prairie? What would a wolf do in the water, or a beaver in the desert?"

Young Messenger sighed. "Do you think that I could live all my life here?"

At this, she gave him the same fixed sort of look with which she had received him when he first returned to the tepee.

"Were you happier among the whites?" she asked him, pointblank.

"Happy?" exclaimed Messenger.

He drew in a long breath. But he did not answer, for the question made his brain whirl.

A moment later, their talk was interrupted by a noisy shouting of many voices on the edge of the camp, a sound that rolled rapidly up until it reached the lodge of War Lance. Into the dwelling came Bray and old Lessing, in high excitement.

"Here's War Lance coming," said Bray, "and he has the answer from that sneakin' crook, Summer Day."

"What is it?" exclaimed the squaw. "What will he do, now? Does he still say that the Iron Hand is a young boy without a name?"

"You'll hear it in a minute," said Lessing. "Messenger, it's crooked business. Mark you that! Crooked business as sure as my name is Hank Lessing!"

War Lance in person entered the lodge a moment later.

He did not hurry to give his message, but first greeted his guests and then sat down with his usual dignity and lighted a pipe, ceremonially. It was only after a long moment that he said in his deep voice: "This is the way in which Summer Day speaks. He says: 'The young white boy is driven to his death by a wicked spirit. I have tried to keep him from harm, but he will not listen to me. The evil spirit is stronger in him than good sense.

"'If he wishes to meet me, let us meet alone.

"'I hear a name ringing in my mind. It is the canyon of

the Mighty Voice. Let us both ride into the canyon on the next day. Let us go into it in the afternoon, just after the sun has started toward the west. There we shall meet and while the Water People are singing, we shall fight.

"'If the Iron Hand is afraid to do this, let the Blackfeet know that he is a woman, and send him away from their lodges. If he will meet with me there, let him come alone. Let him take an oath that no Blackfeet will ride with him, and I shall take an oath that no Blackfeet will ride with me. Let him make a vow that he will not permit a Blackfoot warrior to be with him, or near him to help, and I shall take the same oath before the chiefs, and the old men of the tribe. Then I shall ride into the canyon of the Mighty Voice, and the Sky People help the young man, for help he will need!'"

When War Lance had finished repeating this long message, word by word, he resumed the smoking of his pipe, puckering his brow above it, in deep thought.

"You ain't gunna go," said Lessing to the boy. "You listen to me, lad. You ain't gunna go. Not till I've gone and scouted that canyon and seen that it's safe. Because Summer Day wouldn't take a risk with you. Not after what you done in the neck of the pass, lately. No Indian would take a chance with you, man to man, unless he was a fool, and nobody could ever accuse Summer Day of bein' that!"

Messenger listened, but he did not answer. Instead, he turned to the thoughtful chief and asked: "What would you do, War Lance?"

The other shook his head.

"Summer Day has a very strong medicine, but so has my brother with the Iron Hand. If there is to be a fight, why will he not fight where many warriors may stand by and look on? What harm do eyes do him? He has done his magic a great many times before the eyes of all the people. We have seen him call the rain, and it fell. We have heard him ask the thunder to speak, and it has spoken. Now, then, why should we not be allowed to see his battle magic, also? If he is going to call up spirits from underground, or bring them down from the sky, let us all watch him do it. But if there is something else in his mind, then that is a bad thing."

"What else could be in his mind?" asked the boy.

"A jack rabbit runs faster than a coyote, but coyotes eat many rabbits," declared the chief. "And that is because they use their wits, for their wits are sharper than their teeth, by a great deal. How will Summer Day use his wits, which are still sharper than the coyote's?"

"What would you do, then?" asked the boy.

"I would send back an answer and say that you are very glad to ride into the canyon of the Mighty Voice to meet him, or into any other canyon, for that matter, and that you do not want any Blackfoot warriors to help you. But you want to take in ten famous braves so that they may see the great enchantments of Summer Day, because in spite of those enchantments you intend to kill him, as hungry people kill a fat dog!"

His voice rose as he spoke. And every one in the tepee nodded in assent.

"There'll be a trick! There'll be a trick!" exclaimed the trapper. "Oh, he's a fox, that Summer Day. He's killed more men by craft than War Lance has ever killed by open fighting!"

"What can he do?" asked the boy. "He takes an oath before the old men not to bring in helpers. Isn't that enough of a surety for me? Will he break the oath?"

"Not in a million years," answered the trapper. "But he might find some way of slippin' around it. Take my advice, and Bray's advice, and the advice of War Lance, and don't you go near to that canyon of the Mighty Voice!"

"Aye," said Bray, "you keep away from that. I don't want

to go back to Fort Lippewan and tell that gent that you've gone and disappeared in the canyon of the Mighty Voice."

"Do you think that it would trouble him?" asked young Messenger bitterly.

He took from his pocket the wallet, and from the wallet he took the letter which he had been cherishing so carefully. This letter, to the utter amazement of Lessing, he tore twice in two, and threw it on the fire. Then he turned to War Lance.

But those torn fragments were light, and the upward draft of the heated air just above the fire caused the papers to shelve off to the side and fall to the ground at Lessing's feet. He picked them up, and freshening the fire with some of the wood that was piled near it, he made a gesture as if throwing the papers into the rising smoke and the flames.

Instead, he conveyed them quietly into his pocket.

And, in the meantime, he heard the boy speaking to the war chief.

"My good friend, War Lance, everything that you say is true. It shows me that you are my friend. I think that Summer Day is full of tricks, also, and as you say, his wits may be sharper than a coyote's. But if he can use them to eat me, he is welcome. He is the end of my trail. Whether I win or lose, now, I hardly care. But I am tired of waiting. If you have a fast horse, give him to the messenger, and send him back with news to Summer Day that I will meet him in the canyon."

# 40

No one argued against this decision, because it was spoken in such a way that argument was not possible. Lessing left the lodge almost immediately after, and strolled from the camp into the woods, where the evening was coming down, moist and dark. He found a footstep behind him, and turning, he made out the face and the burly shoulders of Bray, through the dusk. He halted and confronted him.

"It's all right," said Bray. "I ain't here to make any trouble about it, but I hanker after seein' that letter as much as you do, partner."

Lessing nodded.

"I seen that you was watchin'," he admitted. "We'll get a light here, and have a look."

They kindled a small flame and by this light they patched the fragments of the letter together.

Lessing, then, began to read aloud, stumbling a good deal, for he was not very familiar with print, to say nothing of swiftly running handwriting like this one.

The letter began:

MY DEAR BOY:

"This ought to come to you through the hand of your uncle, Thomas Vance. He has undertaken to bring it out along the same Western trail which you were to follow, though you need not be particularly grateful to him for the effort, as will be explained later on.

"It may be that he will not reach you until you have found the Blackfoot beast of an Indian. If the fellow is still alive, I'm convinced that his ugly face will not be very hard to find; and my real hope is that you will have executed your mission before this letter is handed to you. Because, the moment you read this, all the obligation which you have felt ceases. From the moment you read it, you owe nothing to me, and nothing to the dead man.

"This quiet air of Seville has not put my conscience to sleep, as one might have expected. Instead, it has wakened me to a sense of crimes which I knew before, but did not realize.

"My dear lad, you are the one who has been chiefly injured by me. I have done various evil things in my time, but no one have I injured as I have injured you. I have injured you so much that, at a single stroke, I can destroy your nearest relative, as you think. You have thought of me as your father. I now remove your thought. I am not he!

"Who is your father, then, and what is he?

"That I cannot tell you.

"What fiend prevailed upon me to raise you as my son?

"That I shall explain simply.

"When I saw poor Vance lying dead in the little camp, where the brute of a Blackfoot had left him, the dreadful look of his mutilated face made me swear that I would, in some way, take a revenge upon the red monster who had done the thing. And that purpose was boiling in my mind when I left the place. I had buried Vance as well as I was able and put up a headstone, with his name chipped into it. Then I went off, carrying with me the chip of wood with the likeness of the Blackfoot cut upon it.

"I traveled two days—or was it three?—and then I came out on a river and went down to the bank of it for a number of miles until I reached a little cabin, the ashes of which were still smoking. In the ruins, I could see two dead bodies. And while I stood there, I heard a sound like that of a small, helpless animal and ran into the brush and found there a two- or three-year-old boy.

"Now, then, my lad, inspirations of good or of evil will sometimes leap out of a man's mind fully grown. The instant that I looked down on you and thought of your murdered father and mother, that instant I decided that you should become my instrument in exacting vengeance from the Indians.

"Why should I have not taken vengeance with my own hand?

"You know the answer very well. I am not a brave man. I never have been. The frightful truth is that I crouched in the brush and saw the last of the torments of poor Vance, without daring to show myself to the monster of a Blackfoot!

"Now, my boy, you know the worst of it, and instead of regretting, you'll be glad that you are not the son of such a man as I.

"However, I took you back East with me, and there I raised you, for all that you know, as though you were my own son.

"I took a peculiar pleasure in that education.

"I had a right, I felt, to make you a cutting instrument. Your own mother and father had been killed by the Indians. To what better purpose could you devote your life than to a complete revenge. Therefore, I determined that I would make you a white Indian, and send you out to tower like a hawk over small birds.

"The Indians were enduring, indifferent to pain.

"I had you trained in daily torments, until you could smile while your thumb was being torn, or a candle singed you. I trained you to endure cold, heat, hunger, miserable weariness of body and soul. I had experts give you every manual dexterity with weapons. Your boxing teacher enjoyed knocking you down—until you were able to turn the tables on him. Your instructor in firearms never knew how to speak a good word to you.

"'In that hot fire,' I used to say to myself, 'he will have every bit of a weaker metal burned out of him, and he will become the purest steel.'

"Well, you became steel, my boy.

"When you grew older, I finally explained what my purpose had been in making you what I was trying to have you be. I convinced you that there was a holy necessity. I swore that you were the son of my bone and blood, and that all my property would go to you eventually.

"Well, my lad, your so-called uncle, Thomas Vance, finally found out enough to hold a gun to my head. That gun was the danger of a public scandal if he made clear two things: First, that I had acted a long, living lie to you. Second, that I had raised you like a fighting animal.

"Thomas Vance showed me, incidentally, that he did not expect me to live very long, and that he expected a reasonable part of my fortune. His arguments, in short, were convincing, and since I never have been a very bold man, I decided that he was right, and that, therefore, I would have to be wrong.

"There was only one way in which I could recompense you, to

a slight degree, for the harms which I have worked upon you, and that was to tell you the truth. /

"Now you are free to detest and to despise me. But, at least, you are freed also from the dangerous necessity of hunting down the Blackfoot fiend, whoever he may be.

"I must close this letter.

"You no longer are a Messenger. What your true name may be, I cannot tell you. That obscure little cabin in the woods—I don't think that I ever could find it again.

"You have lost me as a father. You have nothing to use in replacing the idea that you have lost except, of course, your own fiction, which will create an honest and strong pioneer for a father, and a beautiful and good woman for a mother.

"No doubt, your imaginings will be right.

"At any rate, at this point I pass out of your life.

"What will become of you, I wonder, and in a rather melancholy sense. But Thomas Vance will have you separated from me. He will not see a penny of the Messenger fortune diverted to false blood. And I cannot fight back or argue against him. Being the strongest, he must be right.

"Good-bye, my lad.

"At least, if I cannot send you money, I can give you to the world as a sword with a cutting edge and a needle point that will stab through a foot of cold steel, without breaking, or marring. There never was another like you, before. There never will be another like you, hereafter, you are unique.

"The best of good fortune come to you. Forgive me if you can, though you will find that hard.

"Always with kind thoughts of you,

"CHARLES MESSENGER."

The trapper, having finished this letter, first crushed it between his hands, and then he dropped it into the dwindling little fire.

"Why, Lessing," said Bray, "maybe the poor kid, he sort of wants to die, after that!"

# 41

That night, young Messenger, if he still had the right even to think of himself under that name, lay down in the roll of buffalo robe which War Lance furnished him and looked steadily up toward the smoke vent at the top of the lodge. It seemed to him that his life had reached the edge of a precipice, and that from it he was about to topple into nothingness.

He had lost his name.

He had lost his total identity.

He discovered that he had given the precious years of a young life to a false goal and to a false ideal.

And, finally, the woman he had found among the savages had thrust him away from her in fear, and in disgust.

He turned these facts slowly through his mind, and closed his determination.

On the morrow, no doubt that the medicine man planned upon some subtle trickery in the ravine of the Mighty Voice. Once before he had met the white lad with gun, knife, and hand. And he would surely not be fool enough to attempt the battle again. There was some resource of cunning upon which he would rely.

Well, he should have his chance.

Young Messenger closed his eyes, and by an effort of his powerful will, he was asleep in an instant.

When he wakened in the morning, he went down to the

river and plunged into the snow-water with the others, and with them he raced up the slope for the village, apparently as lighthearted as ever before. He rode out on a borrowed pony and hunted through the morning with a dozen young braves.

So they came to noon in the day, and then, back at the village, Messenger took another of the ponies of War Lance, who refused all recompense, whether of weapons or hard cash.

"Suppose I had three times a hundred horses," said he, "how would they pay, if I gave them to you, for the glory you have won for me and for all my friends among the Blackfeet?"

He took the hand of the boy, after the white man's fashion, and pressed it with a fervent grip.

Then Messenger went out into the open air and sun, rather glad of the keenness of it against his face, and the bite of it upon his shoulders.

He was dressed all as an Indian, this day. His other clothes, worn to tatters, had had to be discarded, and the squaw of War Lance had managed to find a beautifully cut but simple suit of deerskins.

In this outfit, all that looked strange about him, for the garb, was the shortness of his hair. His skin was altering to the Indian color.

Every man, every women, every child, in that village knew very well why he was riding out and where he was going. He rode the finest pony which the chief could supply, a glorious bay stallion with eye of fire, and a muzzle which could have fitted into a pint pot. Its legs were of hammered steel, and it went like flowing water.

Behind the boy rode War Lance himself, plainly dressed, without a feather in his long hair, and with a look of sadness in his face.

The women, when they saw this attitude of mourning,

set up a wailing cry, which they ceased when the Iron Hand came to the place where the two Crow captives were, in turn, seated upon their horses. In spite of the hurt shoulder of Red Feather, on this day they intended to start out on the long journey toward their own people. Before them Messenger paused, and gave them a cheerful wish for their journey.

Messenger went on, and the women put up their doleful cry again.

When he came to the edge of the village, there he found the eight lifeguards and companions of War Lance ranged in a double file, through which he passed.

They were dressed very splendidly, equipped for the warpath, but their faces were blackened, in token of mourning. Of them, the oldest alone spoke to him saying: "Brother, how gladly would we ride with you. Now may the spirits help you and give you eyes like a hawk to see through the medicine and the enchantments of Summer Day."

He raised his hand to them silently, and with it raised, he passed through that double file and went on over the open, grassy land, and into the woods.

He came to a clearing, and there in the dappling shadows of the leaves, he saw someone on horseback, sitting still as the trees around. It was Yellow Antelope. There was in her face something that strove to speak to him, and that failed. She made a gesture with both her hands, palm up, but Messenger went past her with his eyes fixed sternly ahead.

He had a perfect foreboding that this was to be his last day on earth, and he rode on to meet the end of his life without weakness and without regret.

He had no enthusiasm for the fight. He had no excitement or fear, either. If ever he had his chance to meet the medicine man at close range or at long range, he had not the least doubt that he could conquer, as he had conquered before. But he could guess that Summer Day would not venture on a battle unless he were sure, beforehand, of winning it. There was some contrivance, some stratagem on the way which the famous Blackfoot must have contrived before he asked for the meeting.

So he came, at the last, to the mouth of the canyon of the Mighty Voice.

Its name was well given. For it was a great gorge, running north and south, with huge stone walls on either side, and at the base of these walls a thick apron of soil on which grew enormous trees. All over the central portion of the ravine's floor were scattered boulders as great in size as small houses. And, plunging among these, ran the currents of a powerful stream.

Sometimes the water leaped over a cascade; sometimes it fell with shattering force and a roar into a sheer descent; sometimes it was merely breaking the strength of its body against the boulder faces. But in doing these things, it set up a continual song which was composed of many parts. Thunders, and bellowings, and loud shouting rolled and reechoed up and down the canyon of the Mighty Voice. It was like coming into the presence of a vast chorus which surrounded the listener, and yet obviously the one singer was the white water that flashed through the center of the valley.

The entrance itself was imposing, like the rudiments of a vast natural gate. A dark cliff went up on the left and a light-colored one upon the right. There could hardly have been a more solemn entrance to a more noble graveyard.

Then he passed through, and once fairly inside the canyon, he felt dwarfed and insignificant, and all his life seemed to shrink to a mere pinpoint, without a meaning.

So he went forward, perfectly indifferent to the result, and only instinctively, as he passed along the trail near the edge of the water, looking about him among the boulders.

Then a sudden, thin, small screech reached his ears through the uproar of the water, and he turned suddenly in the saddle.

# 42

It was merely the gray streak of a rabbit that leaped from the covert of a little bush, and bolted in vain, for over it slid a long shadow that launched out from the rock above, and took shape as a wildcat with flattened ears and a gaping mouth.

It scooped up the little fugitive, biting through its life and its death screech with strong jaws. Then, bounding back onto the top of the rock, it looked fiercely over its shoulder toward the boy, while it lashed its sides with its long tail.

The next moment, it had slunk from sight, but young Messenger remained there for a moment, troubled and ill at ease. After all, it is well enough to philosophize about death. In the distance the thing seems not at all overpowering, but at close hand, it is quite another matter. And the yellow glare of the eyes of the cat, and the sinuous grace of the destroying leap, and the last poor cry of the little rabbit remained a picture for the eye and for the ear of the boy.

He went on, but in quite another manner, for now he constantly probed everything about him, with the keenest of eyes. Once he saw a movement at which he almost fired, pointblank—but then he saw that it was merely the reflected light from the face of the stream.

It had given him a start, however. It was enough, in itself, to tell him that his calm had been an affectation, and that life was sweet to him.

There was beauty and splendor in this world. Not a nameless life in the tawny, smoke-stained cities of the East—that was not worth any great effort to retain—but here was a different matter.

The cliffs were so lofty that now, although the sun was still high, the slanting shadows from the western wall had more than covered the floor of the ravine and were climbing gradually up the eastern cliff. The voice of the water was not, it seemed to him now, singing a death chant, but a glorious song of abounding life. The valley floor trembled with the music, and Messenger found himself drawing down deep, quick breaths.

He went on much more slowly, now probing at every suspicious thing with careful eyes.

And suddenly he felt danger behind him! He whirled, throwing himself along the side of his horse as he did so, and swinging the rifle, with one hand, so that it rested across the withers of the horse.

He saw nothing. But something crossed the tail of his eye, he felt, gliding between two big rocks to the rear. He held his difficult position for amother moment. But nothing stirred, and there was no sound to the rear.

Was it a dream?

Then he shook his head, and made himself erect in the saddle again.

Say that he were being followed, say that someone was yonder among rocks that overlooked him, then certainly he would have been fired upon before this.

With a wave of self-contempt, Messenger banished all

care, for the moment, of what might be happening behind him, and attended to what was ahead.

Now he came out into a small hollow.

It was a steep-sided dip both before him and upon the farther side. The bottom was flat and bare except for a little nest of boulders in the midst. Moving ice sheets, perhaps, had gouged out this depression. To the left ran the water in a white, straight rush of foam.

He considered crossing the hollow. It was dangerously open, but to turn to the side and work around through the boulders, though safer, would be wearisome work.

And he was young. He was very young, and, therefore, very careless. He gave the problem a single moment of thought and then pushed his stallion forward. It started and, in a moment, was skidding through a few small stones and gravel but keeping its balance perfectly.

So they came to the bottom and saw that, on the farther side, the ascent was far less steep. Messenger would be across and up it, in a moment!

So he gave the good stallion the rein and went on until the hard rocks began to slope up once more. In the meantime, he had been scanning the boulders that crowned like battlements the rim of the hollow, and nothing suspicious was seen. Yet, straight before him, there was the sudden clang of a rifle.

He had been leaning, that instant, to arrange the stirrup; and, at the sound of the shot, the stallion bounded violently to the side.

Of what use, then, were all the long lessons in horsemanship which he had taken? He was flipped from the saddle like a stone, and instantly he heard a triumphant war whoop before him.

He lay flat, half stunned, and looking up, he saw above a nest of rocks a feathered head rising, and the dark face of an

Indian, then the whole body to the waist, and the hands holding a rifle.

But, miracles of miracles, it was not the medicine man— it was not Summer Day. Instead, if the arrangement of that feathered headdress meant anything, this was a Crow warrior.

He snatched up his rifle, and still lying flat, put in a snap shot. There was a *yip* of alarm and surprise from the other. Apparently he had thought that his shot had driven straight through the body of the white man, and that this was what had sent him to the ground. Now, starting back, the Crow tumbled out of sight, his voice still babbling out excited words.

The next instant, something that was not water hit the rock three inches from the face of Messenger, and stung his cheek with the molten rays which splashed from it. The report of a rifle directly behind him immediately followed, and he whirled to his feet.

As he did so, another bullet cut the air with the sound of a wasp, blowing down a strong wind, and he heard the report of a rifle from the eastern rim of the hollow.

Then he understood.

How simple, like the explanation of all riddles, was this one! For the medicine man had simply called for an oath that no Blackfoot would follow either of them into the fight, and no Blackfeet were there. Instead, he had merely applied to some roving Crows.

Would they not be delighted to have the hero of the night battle, the Iron Hand, delivered up to them? The matter could not have been clearer, and the hollow into which he had blundered so blindly was rimmed with Crow warriors!

Now another and another puff of smoke bloomed like little translucent white flowers on the edge of the hollow, north and south; but by this time he was running, and those good marksmen missed each time, though so narrowly that he always heard the whistling of the bullet.

They had him most hopelessly trapped. There was nothing for him, then, except to take what shelter he could find in the open nest of the rocks. There he could at least lie down and gain some shelter.

He reached them, and flung himself flat just as another ball sung past his shoulder. He was safe, but safe for no more than a moment. Sooner or later, they would get the accurate range, and then they would surely get at him through the wide interstices of the stone, or with a plunging fire from either side.

He lay there, panting, and heard the ringing hoofs of his horse, as the animal galloped to a distance.

There was the river water as a possible means of escape. He might run to it and throw himself in, trusting his life to the speed of the currents. But when he ventured a glance in that direction, he saw the water churning among the rocks, heard it roaring, and knew very well that he could not live ten seconds in that sweep of water constantly set with rocky teeth.

What could he do, then?

There was nothing except a desperate charge. But a charge was the most foolish thing of all, for the sharp slope, all around him, would be sure to stop him to a crawling pace, and he could be shot down with consummate ease.

Then the firing stopped for a moment, and he heard a high-pitched voice call out: "Iron Hand! Iron Hand!"

It was in the Blackfoot tongue, and he thought surely that he could recognize the unforgotten accents of the medicine man.

"Iron Hand!" went on the other, his notes cutting clearly through the air and reaching the ear of the boy. "Now you have ridden on your last trail. Iron Hand, stand up, and walk out into the sun, leaving your rifle and your pistol behind you. We will let you become a prisoner. Do you hear me? The Crows who are with me will let you become their prisoner."

Messenger listened, and smiled a little to himself, but a shudder followed, for he could hear the high-pitched laughter of the medicine man floating over the hollow like the triumphant screaming of a bird of prey.

He did not answer.

If the stones about him had been a foot higher, he could have found a secure shelter among them, but as it was—a bullet beat with a heavy stroke against the face of the stone where he was lying. So he wriggled across to the other side, only to have his face filled with rock splinters as a shot from the opposite direction clipped under his head.

He was lost!

# 43

They would torture him to death, the bullets striking him again and again, until one of them reached a vital spot. But perhaps he could exact some retribution from them, and staring through a gap in the rocks, rifle in hand, he saw a dark form appear suddenly beside one of the rocks at the eastern side of the rim of the hollow. He could thank his teachers of the old days for their long instructions in the estimation of distance. It might be two hundred or a hundred and eighty yards, and instantly his gun was at his shoulder. He saw the little puff of smoke and heard the bullet sing close above him. The Crow stooped toward shelter, and at that instant the boy drew his bead and curled his forefinger gently with a pressure of his whole hand, over the trigger.

The explosion kicked up the muzzle of the weapon a little, and then, with a savage grin of satisfaction, he saw the brave straighten, make two or three staggering steps, and finally topple headlong from the rock. The body struck the sloping side, bounded like a thing made of rubber, and then tumbled head over heels to the bottom of the slope, where it lay, a still and shapeless heap.

And there was some meager satisfaction in this. Let them show themselves with more care, if they expected to hunt him to the death! Aye, they would be wary, now, how they so much as showed a head or a hand above the surrounding rock. The yell of rage that came wailing over the hollow was the sweetest satisfaction to him.

There were many feathers in the headdress of that warrior. A chief, perhaps?

Aye, but those feathers were not of the Crow mode. They were far more familiar. They were Blackfoot, in fact.

And the boy almost leaped to his feet. It was Summer Day. It could be no other. An almost chance shot had accomplished his mission for him in the midst of the fight. The others were by no means giving up the struggle, however. The rifles clanged in rapid succession. Something ripped across the calf of his leg like a red-hot iron.

Then a great voice boomed across that shallow valley.

It was a language which he did not understand, akin to the Blackfoot, but not the Blackfoot dialect, in fact. Then he could see the speaker, mounted on the top of a high rock, just to the south of the hollow. He was a tall Indian, one arm close to his side—yes, it was bound there with a bandage, and in another moment the boy had recognized Red Feather.

It seemed that the chief was haranguing the empty air, for all the answer he got, but never was Messenger so glad to hear any voice; for he knew that those words from their famous war chief were sending back the Crow warriors who had come into the canyon to strike a celebrated coup.

Messenger stood up.

Not only had the certainty of death been removed from him, but a new joy ran suddenly through his veins. Staring toward the rock rim where the chief stood, he saw Bray and Lessing come suddenly out from among the boulders. They waved down to him, and he laughed happily and waved back.

They were the shadows whom he had truly felt following him down the ravine. But they had been friends, and not enemies. In the very nick of time they had come secretly up behind him, and one shout from Red Feather was enough to scatter the Crow rascals. There was Straight Arrow also, perched on another rock, and shouting.

He waved back to these doubly welcome friends, and then crossed the hollow to the place where the medicine man lay. He remembered, then, that this fellow, brute as he had been, belonged to the same tribe as War Lance. So he turned the body properly on its back, and folded the arms across the breast. The face of Summer Day had not been injured in the fall from the height, and the same leering smile which it had worn in life was on it now. His rifle lay not far off. And the boy put it beside the fallen warrior. Touching the body with instinctive horror, he closed his eyes, and a breath of wind stirring the feathers at that moment gave Messenger a ghostly feeling that the dead man had nodded, as though in acquiescence to his fate.

The stallion was then soon caught, and zigzagging up the slope brought Messenger again to the rim of the hollow, where he found the whole group around him—Red

Feather, Straight Arrow, Bray, Lessing. He tried to speak out his thanks, but gratitude swelled in the hollow of his throat and choked him. Then the sound of a horse galloping down the rocky ravine reached his ears, and he pointed after it, with an inquiring air. Had one of them lost his horse?

They merely smiled, and looked wisely at one another.

"There goes the man whom you must thank," said Red Feather. "There he runs away from your words, the man who brought us all together and explained that since we were not Blackfeet, we had a right at least to go behind you and guard your back."

"Who is he?" asked the boy, eagerly.

But they only smiled again, and since at that moment the echoing of the hoofbeats rang clearly up to them along the valley, he drove his heels suddenly into the flanks of the stallion and made the good horse fly in pursuit.

Who could it be that had done the thing?

Well, whoever it was would have to ride hard and brilliantly to escape from his pursuit, for the stallion went like a racer.

It was not long before he had a vague glimpse of the fugitive. A small man, he would say. He threw his weight forward, and jockeying the stallion to the utmost speed, he swept into the last stretch that led toward the lofty gates of the ravine.

And there, just before him, urging a swift pinto to its top gait, was Yellow Antelope!

She threw a frightened glance behind and shouted to her horse, but the big stallion swept easily up beside them, and the hands of Messenger pulled the pinto to a stop.

"Yellow Antelope," gasped the boy, "you have run away from me, but I think that after today you will never be able to escape from me again."

And suddenly her glance wavered, and she began to

laugh, though there was a tremor in her voice. At that, he leaned from the saddle and took her in his powerful hands, and held her before him on the stallion.

"Now look at me," he sternly commanded.

"Yes," said she, but still her glance wavered away toward the leaping and the thunder of the water.

"Tell me, Yellow Antelope, why you said 'No' to me that other day by the river?"

"Because," she answered slowly, "I am a Blackfoot, and I cannot be a white man's wife. And I knew that you only had come to us in order to find Summer Day and kill him because of a cruel thing he had done many years ago."

"Then why," he persisted, "do you let me hold you in my arms, and why do you smile at me?"

"Because," said she, "even after you had killed that wicked man, you came so swiftly after me that I began to think that perhaps it was not only Summer Day, after all, who kept you here with the tribe, but that you might stay even for the sake of your friends—such as War Lance, and all the young braves. And even a little for my sake, also."

He smiled down at her with a sort of stern joy.

"Shall I tell you something?"

"Aye," said she.

"The white man who came with Two Buffalo is waiting for an answer to take back to a man who once filled up the whole world for me. He was the greatest thing under the sky.

"The answer I am going to send back is this: 'My friend, all the evil things you have done to me have turned out to be good things, in the end. You sent me out to kill a murderer. He is dead. So is my old self dead. Because I have found my people, and my wife among them!' Can you believe that?"

"Ah," said she, "but your wife for how long? For a year? For two years? Well, it will have to be enough. I shall close

218

my eyes to everything except today and tomorrow, and never dare to look ahead."

"My wife forever," said the boy, in answer.

"And all the friends of your life as white man?"

"I have no friends," he answered her. "I have killed Summer Day. Nevertheless, he had a strong medicine, and I am dead, also. I am so dead, Yellow Antelope, that I have lost my other name, and I have nothing to call myself except the Iron Hand. And that is only in good Blackfoot!"

The stallion began to move forward slowly, as the boy spoke, and he carried the girl and the Iron Hand quietly through the great rude pillars of the gate to the Mighty Voice. Once they were past it, they came out on a hill where the westering sun caught them in a warm tide. And the Iron Hand looked over a glorious green sea of trees, and of rolling, grassy hills, and the gleam of the river went swiftly among them, like a saber stroke. He looked over this great and lovely country and began to laugh, though he was almost as close to tears as to mirth. But the girl, looking constantly up to his face, understood, and was content.